Escape on the Underground Railroad

Liberty Letters®

Escape on the Underground Railroad

Nancy LeSourd

ZONDERVAN.com/
AUTHORTRACKER
follow your favorite authors

www.zonderkidz.com

Escape on the Underground Railroad
Previously published as *The Personal Correspondence of Hannah Brown and Sarah Smith*
Copyright © 2003, 2008 by Nancy Oliver LeSourd

Requests for information should be addressed to:
Zonderkidz, Grand Rapids, Michigan 49530

Library of Congress Cataloging-in-Publication Data

LeSourd, Nancy.
   Escape on the Underground Railroad / by Nancy LeSourd.
      p. cm. -- (Liberty letters).
   A revised edition of a work originally published in 2003 by Zonderkidz under title: Personal
correspondence of Hannah Brown and Sarah Smith.
      Summary: Letters between two young girls, one from Goose Creek, Virginia, and her
friend living in Philadelphia, chronicle their involvement in helping an escaped slave travel via
the Underground Railroad to join her father in Canada.
    ISBN 978-0-310-71391-3 (softcover)
    1. Underground Railroad--Juvenile fiction. [1. Underground Railroad--Fiction. 2. Fugitive
slaves--Fiction. 3. Slavery--Fiction. 4. Christian life--Fiction. 5. Letters--Fiction.] I. LeSourd,
Nancy. Personal correspondence of Hannah Brown and Sarah Smith. II. Title.
   PZ7.L56268Es 2008
   [Fic]--dc22

2008015008

Editor: Barbara Scott
Art direction & cover design: Merit Alderink
Interior design: Carlos Eluterio Estrada
Cover illustrator: Guy Porfirio

Printed in the United States of America

08 09 10 11 12 • 5 4 3 2 1

For Cate and Luke

Philadelphia, Pennsylvania

FOURTH MONTH 27, 1858

Dear Hannah,

I've done it again. This is the third time in as many months that I've brought it up. It was no sooner out of my mouth than I wished I could take it back.

I graduate from Friends Central High in two years, and if I am going to enter Female Medical College, I need to study physiology now. There is so much to learn. And what I really need is a skeleton. So, I asked my parents. Again. For the third time. Big mistake.

Father rambled on about a proper Quaker woman's aspirations. You know, husband, children, home, and service. I reminded him that the Medical College was started by Quakers for Quaker women, and that I could serve by healing others, but he pretended he didn't hear me.

Mother put down her stitching and simply said, "There will be no dead bones in this home."

I promised her Friend Bones (as I like to call him just as I would any other beloved Quaker friend) would be very well behaved. "Friend Bones won't rattle around because I'll hang him from a pole in my room so I can study him better."

Mother tilted her head and began to answer. She stopped short and studied me. It was almost as if she were going to relent, but then, me and my big mouth, I had to fill the silence, didn't I? "Friend Bones," I blurted out, "will be quite at home here. Like one of the family." Mother got up, said she had washing to do, and that was that.

Sometimes I think Father regrets bringing me home from Springdale Boarding School right next door to you and enrolling me at Friends Central High, here in the city. Although Father definitely believes in the equality of all men, regardless of race, I'm

not sure he agrees that applies to equality of all men *and women*. Father is not comfortable with the idea of a woman being a doctor.

At the rate I am going, however, it will be a long time before I can become a doctor. Friends Central doesn't offer more-advanced science courses. I guess I shouldn't complain though. Even the boys can't take physiology.

When I'm not pestering my parents about Friend Bones, we spend more and more time working together on getting delivery packages safely to their destinations. Yet, it's more dangerous now than ever to be in the delivery business. And complicated. There are many who would see us fail. The stakes are much higher now — with grave penalties. Ask your grandfather to explain. I should close for now.

Your friend,
Sarah

Goose Creek, Virginia

SIXTH MONTH 2, 1858

Dear Sarah,

I helped Grandfather survey another road today. His map of Loudoun County has been well received and he wants to get this next map published soon. I hope so, because he might take me with him to visit his publisher in Philadelphia ... and you!

Joshua came along again to help. He's seventeen and is Uncle Richard's apprentice at the foundry. Although he is only a year older than I am, our lives are so different. He's been an orphan for twelve years now, and ever since, he has had to work to earn his food and lodging.

As usual, I kept the notebook and carefully wrote down everything Grandfather called out to me as he and Joshua worked the chain and compass to measure the road. Joshua and Grandfather can make calculations in their heads faster than I can write them down.

I waited for my chance. When Joshua started to roll up the surveying chain, I showed Grandfather your letter. He read it quickly, then glanced at Joshua, and whispered that I was not to say a word about this to anyone. On the way home, Joshua tried to make me laugh, but my mind was too preoccupied with questions. What is this delivery business that you're involved in? Why is Grandfather being so mysterious? Why won't he talk about it with Joshua around?

After supper, Grandfather asked me to come to the barn with him to brush down Frank. You remember Frank, don't you? Such a solid horse, deserving of such a solid name. Grandfather brushed away some of the hay in Frank's stall and showed me a trapdoor.

Grandfather did not say a word. He just let me look inside with my lamp. I saw a bed of straw and a blanket. I stared inside for a long time. Then Grandfather lowered the trapdoor and spread the hay over it again. Frank nuzzled me, but I could not move. I shivered in the night air even though it was quite warm. Thoughts, questions whirled around in my head.

Grandfather put his hands on my shoulders and said, "The Lord said he came to proclaim liberty to the captives — to set free those in bondage. How can we do any less?" He glanced over his shoulder and continued, "It is fourteen miles from our home to the Potomac River. Once a slave crosses that river, it is but a short journey through Maryland to Pennsylvania … and freedom."

We walked back to the house in silence. Then I lit my candle stub and came straight to my room to write this letter. I know many of our faith are part of what they call the Underground Railroad, but Grandfather? Sarah, is your family part of this Underground Railroad too? Are these the packages you spoke about? Why are you in danger? Don't you live in a free state? How long has Grandfather been hiding slaves right here at Evergreen? Are we in danger too? I have so many questions. I cannot sleep.

> *Your friend,*
> *Hannah*

Philadelphia, Pennsylvania

SIXTH MONTH 14, 1858

Dear Hannah,

I shared your letter with Mother. She says we must not speak of such things by letter, especially by any letter posted in Virginia. She has a plan, though. Your grandfather arrives tomorrow. I'll send a special present back with him for you.

I have worked my fingers to the bone sewing all week. We need shirts, lots of shirts. I'll explain more later. Hannah, I'm afraid that our friendship quilt must wait a bit longer. There is not time right now to work on it.

I had a brilliant idea to win Father over about Friend Bones. I think he's worried I want to live in a man's world and am not dedicated to becoming a proper Quaker woman. So, today I rode the horse-drawn omnibus to Forty-Fourth and Haverford to volunteer at the Association for the Care of Colored Orphans. Right now there are 67 boys and girls, from babies to nine year olds, living at the Shelter.

I asked the director if I could help with nursing the children when they are sick. Sounds noble, but I figured that with this many children here, the doctor is likely to stop by often. So, maybe I could learn medicine while I help out. Mrs. Whitaker said right now she needs my help to tutor the older children in reading, writing, and basic computations.

Mrs. Whitaker told me about a new boy who arrived last week. He's seven years old, and his name is Zebulon Coleman. I glanced in his direction. "He seems scared," I commented.

Mrs. Whitaker nodded. "The children are often frightened when they first arrive. New surroundings. New people." She lowered her voice to a whisper. "Something terrible happened to Zebulon's parents, so he may need more time to adjust."

I started to ask her what happened, but she turned and walked over to Zebulon to introduce him to me.

Zebulon didn't speak when I greeted him. He lowered his eyes and stared at the same spot on the floor. I tried my best to let him know I was friendly, but his eyes didn't budge.

I wonder what happened to Zebulon's family.

On the way out, I bumped into a man with a suitcase. He tipped his hat and said, "Peter Pennington, at your service."

I said hello but felt uneasy.

He continued, "New girl, eh? Going to help out?"

I brushed past him without an answer. How did he know who I was? What business is it of his anyway? Who is this man? I hope he isn't staying here.

Your friend,

Sarah

Goose Creek, Virginia

SIXTH MONTH 25, 1858

Dear Sarah,

As soon as Grandfather arrived home, I asked about my present from you. He smiled and handed me a little seedling in a big clay pot. Not exactly what I was expecting from my best friend. You know I can get tree seedlings from Grandfather's nursery any time I want.

After a few moments he said, "Hannah, thee is so disappointed! Come with me. There is more to this little seedling than meets the eye."

Grandfather led me to a table in the greenhouse and turned the pot upside down. All the dirt not attached to the roots rolled out onto the table, as did a small leather pouch. Inside were your letters!

What a magnificent idea your mother had to hide your letters in a pot. Now when I write back, Grandfather will carry my letters to you the same way. It's just another pot with other cuttings from our nursery here at Evergreen to sell in Philadelphia. No one will ever guess our secret. If we must speak about things better left unspoken, this will do quite nicely.

Grandfather had another surprise for me. A buyer for the cuttings from the Ginko tree did not have enough cash to make the purchase. Instead, he opened a velvet pouch of pearls and other gems. Grandfather selected a perfect, milky white pearl in payment. He said that when he saw it, he thought of me and wanted me to have this as a token of his love for me.

Have you worked on our friendship quilt lately? I will take my leather pouch to bed tonight and read your letters by candlelight.

Your friend,
Hannah

Philadelphia, Pennsylvania

SIXTH MONTH 28, 1858

Dear Hannah,

By now you have my letters in hand. Were you surprised? It's a lot to think about, I know. There's more you need to know.

One night while your grandfather was here, Mr. Robert Purvis from the Anti-Slavery Vigilance Committee came to speak with Father about a package that was delivered here for our care—a slave from Maryland who escaped two weeks ago. Mother and I sat quietly, mending shirts for the fugitives, and listened intently to the men as they talked.

Ever since the passage of the Fugitive Slave Act, fugitive slaves who live in free states can be recaptured and sent back to slavery. The Committee works harder than ever now to get the escaped slaves all the way to Canada.

The slave catchers pay for information to identify a fugitive slave who is now working in the city. The Committee has to be even more careful in order to keep a runaway here in the city. Names must be changed, and sometimes even that isn't enough. Now, more than ever, you've got to know who can be trusted.

Your grandfather said it's harder than ever to help slaves to freedom in Virginia too. As the largest slave state in the country, the Virginia plantation owners are known to help slave owners from other states find their "property" that has escaped north.

He told us that for several months now the slave catchers and their hounds come by Evergreen routinely. He suspects that it is more an attempt to scare him, but your grandfather does not frighten easily. He told us that sheriffs in Culpeper tell these slave catchers it is well known that if a slave makes it to Evergreen, he will make it to freedom. Father and Mr. Purvis laughed because, well, it is true!

Mr. Purvis encouraged your grandfather to step up his efforts,

because now more than ever, the Railroad must operate quickly. The demand is great and experienced conductors who can be trusted are valuable to the movement. Mr. Purvis said he firmly believes that the skill your grandfather has in mapmaking was given to him by God to assist those in bondage.

Father said your grandfather knows every road, path, canal, and creek in Loudoun County, and if anyone can help slaves in their run to freedom, it is Friend Yardley Taylor.

Your grandfather may need your help. After Mr. Purvis left, your grandfather said his hearing is not what it used to be. He said he needs to be nimble to help the slaves but that carting around his heavy, awkward ear trumpet to be able to hear slows him down.

Now that he has shown you the hiding place, you have a special responsibility to ask God what he would have you do with this knowledge. When your grandfather showed you the straw bed, did you not think of the comfort of your own bed with its pillow? When your grandfather showed you the blanket just big enough to cover the straw bed, did you not think of your own ample covers and warm fire inside? Can you turn away from those God brings to your door at Evergreen? Hannah, I hope I have not offended you. But you have a good heart and you must think about what I have said.

I took the omnibus to the Shelter this afternoon. Mrs. Whitaker told me she wants me to work mostly with Zebulon. He was part of a small group of slaves who escaped from Alabama. The Committee split up the ones who made it this far to send them on to Canada by way of various delivery stations. Zebulon will stay here, at least until he is nine. Then they will find work for him so he can learn a skill and have a place to live until he is eighteen.

I asked Mrs. Whitaker what happened to Zebulon's parents, but she only said, "It's a very difficult story—one I will tell you when the time is right. Just know this. Zebulon needs to know you can be a true friend to him."

I don't know how I can show him I am his friend if he won't even talk to me. I tried to get Zebulon to respond to me, but he won't even look at me. He shied away from me when I came close.

I pulled up a chair and sat as close to him as he would allow, and began to read a story out loud with as much expression and enthusiasm as I could. About halfway through the story, I saw him look up at me out of the corner of his eye. When I met his gaze, however, he went right back to staring at the floor.

I kept my eyes on the pages of the book. When I sensed he was looking at me again, I shifted my position so that Zebulon could see the pictures in the book while I read the story. I didn't dare look directly at him. He leaned in a bit. Too soon the story was finished and Zebulon scurried away without a sound.

Oh Hannah, there is just something about that little boy. I must reach him.

On the way out, I almost ran into Peter Pennington. "Good day," he said. He whisked past me and called out for Mrs. Whitaker. I decided to stay and find out what he wanted. I hung back and watched him open his suitcase and begin to pull out lots of different objects. Bars of soap, candles of various sizes, sealing wax, envelopes, writing paper, socks, knitting needles, yarn, sewing thread and needles. So, he's a peddler. Still, the man gives me the creeps. I don't like him.

Your friend,

Sarah

Goose Creek, Virginia

Seventh Month 1, 1858

Dear Sarah,

What are you talking about? Slave patrols? At Evergreen? I haven't seen any slave patrols. Perhaps I don't want to. I know I've heard dogs at night, but I never thought they could be slave patrols. You've told me more about Grandfather's railroad business than he has. But I really don't want to know about it at all—from you or Grandfather.

I like my life the way it is. Simple. Predictable. Safe! Nothing but chores and cooking, school and surveying. You'll see. Wait until I tell you about my day. It's a simple life. There's no danger and no excitement—except for the hogs.

Our fire had gone out overnight. Mother sent me to Springdale Boarding School for some fire early this morning after I finished milking the cows.

Then I churned the butter. I have never minded milking the cows, but the steady pounding and repetition of making butter in the churn is so tiresome. What the cow gives in minutes takes hours of churning. Best to just drink the milk, I say.

We had a lot of baking to do for the picnic this week. We made seven pies out of the dewberries, gooseberries, and peaches I picked yesterday.

This afternoon, I gathered an armload of corn from the corncrib and began to call for the hogs. "P-o-o-o-e. P-o-o-o-e. P-o-o-o-e." The hogs were rooting around in the leaves on the ground for food, but when they heard me, they poked their noses up in the air, sniffed, and then came tearing down the hill. Their snorting and squealing filled the air. Three of them galloped down the hill so fast, they began to bump against each other.

I laughed so hard that I didn't jump out of the way soon enough, and the hogs knocked me down. The corn flew up in the air and

scattered on the ground around me. I brushed myself off and rubbed my poor bruised leg, but I could not stop laughing.

That is, until I saw Joshua standing there, pretending to talk to Father. I could see his shoulders shaking from trying not to laugh. Father's too. I was so embarrassed. Joshua greeted me and picked a twig out of my hair. I felt my face turn hot, and asked him if he would like a piece of pie.

I poured Joshua a tall mug of milk and set a piece of gooseberry pie down on the table in front of him. In minutes the pie was gone. I sliced another piece for him, and as he ate, he complimented my cooking. I admit that I was pleased.

We talked about his work with Uncle Richard at the foundry and surveying with Grandfather. He asked me about Goose Creek School and my friends. I told him about you — well not everything, but about how we got to know each other when you were a boarding student at Springdale. I didn't talk about the deliveries or the packages. I have no idea what Joshua thinks about slavery. He never speaks of slavery — for or against. Of course, I do not ask either.

I surprised myself at my boldness when I asked Joshua, "What does it feel like to be an orphan?"

He responded, "What does it feel like to have loving parents?" Seeing my confusion, he continued, "For me it's all I remember. Just as for you the love of your mother and father is all you have known. But because we both trust in the Lord, one way of living is not better than the other."

I said, "I'm sorry, but I am not sure I understand you."

He explained, "I have always experienced God's care in all my affairs. He has led me and continues to show me his fatherly care even though my mother and father are dead. You have experienced the tender mercies of God in the form of a beloved mother and father. Don't we have the same thing to rejoice about — the way God has watched over us, for me directly and for you through your parents? Yet both of us experience God directing and guiding our lives."

I wish I had the confidence Joshua does that God is directing my life. I feel as though one day slides into the next, with the same tasks and chores before me. I know that my training is for a domestic life, with a husband and children, which will likely be mine one day in the future.

Joshua reminds me of you. You are so sure of the calling of God in your life to be a doctor and God's call of your family toward this Railroad business. I, however, am angry at this Underground Railroad interfering with our lives. It's like we have a family secret, but I can't share it with anyone but you. And I'd rather not even know about this secret at all. I just want things to stay the same as they were last year.

Your friend,
Hannah

Goose Creek, Virginia

SEVENTH MONTH 5, 1858

Dear Sarah,

Today at the picnic on the Meeting House grounds, several men got into a loud argument. One man wagged his finger in Grandfather's face and told him he needs to be more cautious about the letters he sends to the newspaper. Joshua stood nearby, watching, taking it all in.

Mother whispered that Grandfather had written the *Sentinel* a letter, which was not only published here, but then was reprinted in the *New York Evening Post*. She explained that some people believe he should not be so public about his position on the Fugitive Slave Act.

Grandfather drew himself up to his full height and said, "If a man doesn't want to read truth in the newspaper, then he should use it to wrap fish." Then he added, "If I am willing to accept the penalty, then I shall continue to follow my convictions."

One of the men argued, "But Friend Yardley, that could mean jail. What good will your opinions be there?"

Jail! What is Grandfather thinking! I'll tell you what I think. I think Grandfather is too outspoken about his anti-slavery views in these perilous times. It is better to keep these things to oneself. Until last month I had no knowledge my family was involved at all, much less here at Evergreen. I have this terrible feeling I keep trying to push way down inside. I'm afraid things are going to change—and not for the better.

Your friend,
Hannah

Philadelphia, Pennsylvania

SEVENTH MONTH 8, 1858

Dear Hannah,

I went back to the Shelter today. Zebulon was just finishing his bath, and Mrs. Whitaker asked me if I would help him out of the washtub and into clean clothes. His eyes flickered for a moment as if he seemed glad to see me, or perhaps that was my wishful thinking.

I wrapped Zebulon in a large towel and pulled him onto my lap to dry him off. He still didn't look at me. He winced as I began to dry his back. There were bloodstains on the towel. Gently I pulled the towel away from his back. Welts crisscrossed his little back. Some were old scars and some quite fresh.

I called for Mrs. Whitaker. "Look!"

Mrs. Whitaker didn't seem that surprised. "Dr. Dixon comes by tomorrow, so until then, let's bind up his wounds as best we can." A few minutes later, she brought ointment and clean strips of cloth and a bowl of warm water. "Zebulon, Sarah will hold you. I just want to clean this up a bit."

Mrs. Whitaker washed the wounds. Zebulon sat on my lap, but still wouldn't look me in the eyes. I watched as the blood and pus oozed onto the wet cloths. When his little body twisted in pain, I reached out to take his hand, and he let me. He squeezed my hand tightly, grimacing against the pain.

Mrs. Whitaker gently applied the salve to Zebulon's wounds. I continued to hold his hand and whispered, "It's going to be all right."

Mrs. Whitaker said, "Dr. Dixon will be here tomorrow and he'll help you feel better."

Zebulon stiffened.

"Mrs. Whitaker, I can come back again tomorrow after school to hold Zebulon while the doctor looks at his back, if that is okay."

When she agreed, Zebulon let out a little sigh. He still won't

look at me, but I think he knows I won't hurt him, and maybe that I won't let anyone else hurt him either.

When Mrs. Whitaker finished dressing his cuts, I gently put a flannel shirt on him, one that was soft and well worn, and buttoned the shirt. Zebulon looked at me, for just a brief moment, hesitated, and then ran off.

How could anyone do this to such a little boy? He's barely seven years old. How could anyone brutally whip a young child over and over again?

Please consider helping your grandfather. I know you must be very careful. It's illegal there in Virginia to even teach a slave to read, much less help a slave escape. I understand that. But it is a horrific business, this buying and selling of humans, and we each have to do something to help.

You and I are from different sides of the Union, though our states almost touch each other. This line between slave and free is one every slave knows only too well. We can't sit by, Hannah, we have to do something.

Devotedly,

Sarah

Philadelphia, Pennsylvania

Seventh Month 9, 1858

Dear Hannah,

Nathaniel came by to call on me today. I'm afraid I was rather curt with him. All I wanted to do was to get back to the Shelter—and to Zebulon. I know what you'd say. My parents too. They think Nathaniel is a perfect suitor. He's a strong student at Friends Central, a devoted member of our meeting, ambitious and college-bound, and would make a good husband.

I want to go to college too. Medical college. There is no time in my life right now for courting, and I can't imagine Nathaniel, or any boy for that matter, wanting to marry a doctor. Besides, I will soon have Friend Bones for a companion.

When I stepped down from the omnibus today, Dr. Dixon walked up to the door of the Shelter holding his medical bag. I hurried to introduce myself. "Dr. Dixon? I'm Sarah Smith. I want to go to the Female Medical College in two years. I'm eager to learn all I can from you."

He looked at me in surprise, and held the door open for me to pass through without saying a word. Mrs. Whitaker greeted him, and pulled him aside to whisper something to him. Probably about Zebulon.

A few minutes later, she motioned to me to come with her and the doctor. I was right. His first patient today would be Zebulon. I took Zebulon by the hand and led him over to Mrs. Whitaker's office.

I lifted Zebulon up onto my lap, and although he wouldn't look at me, he didn't pull away either. I unbuttoned his shirt and slipped it off his shoulders.

I looked up at Dr. Dixon, and he motioned me to take off the bandages. I lifted each one as gently as I could, reassuring Zebulon it would be all right. Some of them were soaked in blood and pus.

Zebulon winced but he looked determined not to cry—not in the presence of this white man.

Dr. Dixon examined the cuts. "The pus is a sign the wound is healing, but it will need some sutures to keep it closed. First we will irrigate the wound and disinfect it with iodine. Then we will stitch this boy up and he'll be right as rain again. Young lady, are you able to assist?"

I gulped. It's one thing to dream about medical college. It's another thing to help stitch up a little boy. Before I could answer, Dr. Dixon opened his medical bag and began to place his tools out on a clean cloth on Mrs. Whitaker's desk. Needles that looked just like sewing needles. Silk thread for the sutures. A glass vial filled with iodine. Mrs. Whitaker brought a bowl of warm water and more clean cloths and set them down by the doctor's instruments.

Mrs. Whitaker asked Zebulon, "Would you like Sarah to help Dr. Dixon?" When he nodded yes, Mrs. Whitaker pulled up another chair. She took Zebulon in her lap with his little legs wrapped around her waist. This exposed his back to Dr. Dixon. Zebulon reached up to put his arms around Mrs. Whitaker's neck.

I whispered, "Zebulon. I'm right here. I'm going to help Dr. Dixon make you all better."

Dr. Dixon began to clean out the wounds. "This cut here is deep, and we will need to do several layers of stitches. Watch what I do, Sarah."

I thought I would be sick watching this, but instead, I was fascinated. I watched everything Dr. Dixon did so skillfully. I handed Dr. Dixon his tools as he asked for them, rethreaded the stitching needle with silk thread, and followed Dr. Dixon's instructions to cut the threads and tie knots in them. It reminded me a lot of mending tears in shirts.

When Dr. Dixon finished, he patted me on the shoulder and said, "Well done." I think that perhaps he said that simply because I didn't faint.

I don't know how he did it, but the whole time Zebulon barely

made a sound. Dr. Dixon asked me to put on the fresh bandages, and he watched as I did so. Afterwards, Mrs. Whitaker gently placed Zebulon down on the floor. He began to walk away, but then turned, and for a brief moment looked at me, and said "Thank you, Miss Sarah." Then, just as suddenly, he slipped away.

Now, more than ever, I want to be a doctor.

Your friend,

Sarah

Goose Creek, Virginia

SEVENTH MONTH 27, 1858

Dear Sarah,

All I have feared has come upon us. Grandfather's life is in danger.

I walked to the store today and waited for Joshua at the corner near Goose Creek School. Joshua was late. Finally I gave up on him and started walking to Purcell's Store.

Then I saw it. A large broadside. Posted on a tree. In big letters at the top it said, "To Yardley Taylor: Chief of the Abolitionist Clan in Loudoun." There it was, for everyone to read.

Listen to what this person said about Grandfather!

"Now look straight down the road leading to Goose Creek—ten to one you will see, emerging from the wood at the end of the lane, a square-built, heavyset, huge-footed, not very courtly figure of an old man, mounted on the vertebra of a somewhat lusty animal, with one hand tightly grasping the rein, and the other hanging on to a little black bag containing the Goose Creek mail."

I could read no further. I was furious. Who was this person calling Grandfather a huge-footed man? Why, my Grandfather is the strongest man I know. The writer even called Frank names! What kind of person begins a letter attacking both man and beast because of the manner in which God has created them?

I ripped the broadside down from the tree. My hands were shaking as I continued to read:

"You declared your innocence of the charge upon which you were arrested and brought to trial—the charge of aiding in the escape of a fugitive slave. But when subjected to the test of a searching examination, you admitted that a runaway slave came to your house. I note it seems rather interesting that all the runaways seem to stumble across your residence. Of course, it is all accidental. You knew him to be a runaway slave, yet you took him in, fed him, and sent him on his way to Pennsylvania rejoicing. And what was your excuse for this offense? That you were acting in conformity with the principles of your faith. This is monstrous! Monstrous!"

The broadside notice told of other attempts Grandfather had made to help slaves escape. It said that Grandfather was arrested before and was tried for his activities! Arrested? I know nothing of this. It must be a mistake.

The broadside said that Grandfather was skillful at managing the Underground Railroad, and that Evergreen was the perfect location for getting slaves through. My heart raced as I read the last line: "Soon, however, that will come to an end."

I ran all the way home and burst through the door. Mother and Father were in the parlor with Grandfather. I thrust the broadside notice into Grandfather's hands and waited. He read it all the way through twice and then gave it to Father and Mother.

I could not stand the silence any longer. "Grandfather, is this true? Were you arrested for helping slaves escape?" His silence told me what I needed to know. I pleaded, "You have to stop. This Underground Railroad business is too dangerous. Let someone else help the runaways get to Pennsylvania."

But Grandfather would hear nothing of it. He believes that God placed him right here at Evergreen precisely because the house is aptly positioned to assist runaways. I know Evergreen is close to the river and helpful to the slaves, but it's still our home. How can Grandfather risk his life and ours?

Mother and Father wanted me to calm down and go back to meet Joshua to walk to Purcell's Store. Joshua would be worried, they said, and we should continue on as if nothing has happened. After all, they said, we should ignore the foolishness of those who would publish their opinions on a tree.

Grandfather said, "I agree with thy parents, but first, Hannah, I have something to ask thee. I need thee to help the slaves who come to Evergreen to make it to freedom. My hearing is not what it used to be. I need to rely on someone young and someone I trust if I'm going to continue to help."

I opened and closed my fists. "Maybe it's a sign from God that you should slow down. Maybe even get out of this business." I was breathing hard, from running home and from my fear. "The slave patrols are already suspicious of you. Now this broadside names our home as a station on the Underground Railroad and you as its chief conductor. It's really not safe here anymore for the slaves."

Grandfather replied, "But the slaves do not know that. They will continue to come to Evergreen, and we must help them."

"No, Grandfather, you must help them. I don't want to hide slaves or help them across the river. It is too dangerous." I glanced at my father, wondering at his silence. "I want things to be the way they were before—before this broadside. Before I knew what you were doing."

Grandfather just stood at the window for the longest time as he looked out on our garden filled with boxwood, lilacs, roses, poppies, peonies, and lilies, many of which he had bought on his trips to Philadelphia.

Then he sighed deeply and said, "Things will never be the same again. Times are changing, Hannah. Thee can sit by and watch it all happen or be part of it. Search thy heart and decide what thee will do. I need help. Will thee help me get the slaves to freedom? Sheriffs and bounty hunters are watching those last miles to the river. It is harder for me to hear the sounds that would warn me to take another path."

Father finally spoke up. "Your mother and I have discussed this and feel that we will all be safer if we work together. Your grandfather is not going to stop doing what he feels called to do, but young ears and eyes could help him stay safe."

Mother nodded. "I trust your life to your grandfather. Yes, he is my father, but I treasure you and I would never put you in his care if I did not know he would protect you."

They all looked at me. Waiting. I could not answer, so I ran out of the room. I feel so ashamed. The whole family is so brave and enthusiastic about this plan—everyone but me, that is. What is the sense of bringing trouble into our home?

Your distressed friend,
Hannah

Philadelphia, Pennsylvania

EIGHTH MONTH 15, 1858

Dear Hannah,

I got your letter and I can tell how confused you are. It's all right. Just take time to think about what you have learned about Evergreen and your family. It's a lot of take in.

I'm sorry I added to your burden by pleading with you to help. I know you'll do the right thing—when the time is right.

Father is quite pleased with my service at the Shelter. He loves to hear my stories about Zebulon, and he had a wonderful suggestion. He thought Zebulon might like a visit to my brother William's farm, Seven Oaks, in Cheltenham. Father thinks Zebulon and Samuel, my nephew, would enjoy each other. Samuel is six years old.

Seven Oaks is just eight miles from the city out Old York Road, and Father thought we could bring back some of the early harvest for the orphanage. I love spending time with William's wife, Graceanna, and she could use my help with Jonathan, who is almost two.

I talked to Mrs. Whitaker, who thought it was a delightful idea. Yesterday, she asked Lionel, a free black who has worked at the Shelter since I've been here, to hitch up the horses to the wagon. It was a beautiful day for the ride to Seven Oaks.

Zebulon and Samuel had so much fun together. The boys loved jumping from one bale of hay to another in the fields. They came in for lunch soaking wet from playing in the creek. I dried them off, taking care with Zebulon's back. He was laughing so hard at Samuel I don't think he noticed any pain as I gently patted his back dry and helped him into one of Samuel's clean shirts. After lunch, they were back in the fields, helping William and Lionel pick some of the late summer produce for the orphanage.

Graceanna and I sat on the porch and watched Jonathan play in the grass with some stacking blocks. "So, any young men in the picture?" she asked.

"There is one who comes to call. Nathaniel Burrows."

"I've heard he's a fine young man and would make a fine husband."

I groaned. "I might like to go to college too, you know. Before I get married."

Graceanna laughed. "Still thinking of becoming a doctor, I see."

"Just think. Free medical care for Samuel and Jonathan!"

"Okay, I'm sold. No more talk about a husband—for today anyway. Have you pestered your Father and Mother for a skeleton lately?"

"No. I'm trying a new tactic. I'm showing Father I can be a good Quaker woman by volunteering at the Shelter. I will ask again later, though."

Then I shared with Graceanna all I knew about Zebulon. "You should bring Zebulon back to be with Samuel soon," said Graceanna. "Here at Seven Oaks he can run around and enjoy his freedom. I imagine that for a boy raised on a plantation, used to blue skies and open fields, an orphanage in a city must seem like a prison."

Lionel and William came in with the boys after loading up the wagon. Lionel said, "Mrs. Whitaker is going to be plum excited to see all this harvest."

I hugged William, Graceanna, and my nephews good-bye. William urged us to come again for another load of food. Zebulon's eyes lit up when Samuel said, "Yes, do come back." Zebulon was so tired that he slept all the way home on a sack of turnips in the back of the wagon.

Your friend,

Sarah

Philadelphia, Pennsylvania

EIGHTH MONTH 22, 1858

Dear Hannah,

Today, some of the girls in my class decided to stop by Friends Central High School to say hello to some of our teachers. The school has grown so much since we moved to our new building at Fifteenth and Race Streets last fall. We've heard there will be over 200 students for this year.

My friend Elizabeth nudged me when she saw a group of boys come out of the school. Nathaniel started down the steps. He looked my way, and gave a nod, but didn't come talk to me.

A few moments later, Principal Ivins (he's principal of the Boys' School) walked down the steps of the school. The boys immediately crowded around him. He's very popular with the boys. The older ones call him Dad.

Nathaniel called out, "Dad, what's $7{,}934 - 1{,}862 \times 2 \div 12$?" Principal Ivins closed his eyes and seconds later, shouted out, "One thousand one hundred twelve!"

The other boys scribbled the computation in the dirt with sticks and much later, called out, "He's right!"

Principal Ivins is a whiz at rapid calculations and no one can beat him. "Now, boys, I'm off to the races!" Principal Ivins exercises his horses about this time every day. The boys begged him to let them come along, and some of the girls called out to come along too. I think they were more interested in the boys than the horses, though.

"Soon enough, young charges," he responded. "Come by Fairmont Park any afternoon next week." With a tip of his hat, he walked briskly down the street.

Some of the boys came over to talk to Elizabeth and the other girls. Nathaniel talked to my friend Lydia for a while. Then he left, walking down the street whistling, without even one glance in my direction.

Elizabeth told me that if I would give him just the least little bit of encouragement, then he might have talked to me instead. I don't know, though. Lydia is very pretty.

I'm excited about school beginning next week. I will take French and Latin, Arithmetic, Chemistry, and Drawing. This year I will have a writing tutorial with Master Eakins.

I told my friends good-bye and went in to see Mrs. Gillingham, the principal of the Girls' School.

"Good day, Mrs. Gillingham. Has the board decided to add physiology classes to the science curriculum this year?"

"No, Sarah," she answered. "There are no new science courses planned for this year. The board may add a physiology course for next year, though."

"That's the best news I've heard in a long time!"

"Sarah, I'm afraid those lectures would only be available to the Boys' School. We are considering adding astronomy classes for the girls." My disappointment must have been fairly obvious because Mrs. Gilligham added, "It is a step in the right direction. You must be patient."

"Mrs. Gillingham, I will be graduated from here before there are real science classes offered to the girls."

Mrs. Gillingham reprimanded me. "Chemistry and physics are real science classes."

"I know. I'm sorry. It's just that I need physiology courses to prepare me for medical college."

"You remind me of a student who graduated from here ten years ago. Her name is Sarah, just like you. Sarah Adamson. She had two uncles who were doctors, and ever since she was a young girl she wanted to be a doctor too. Sarah begged her uncle to take her on as an apprentice. Finally, he relented and agreed."

"What did her parents think about her dreams?" I asked.

"Her father, a true Quaker, wanted to do for his daughter what he would do for a son who wanted to be a doctor. He decided to dedicate part of their home for her studying room. He bought her medical books and a real skeleton."

Sarah Adamson had had a skeleton!

Mrs. Gillingham continued, "After her one year apprenticeship, she applied to medical schools. She was turned down by ten medical colleges, mostly because they did not believe in a woman learning side by side with men. All the medical colleges at that time were only for men. She did not let that stop her. Finally, she found a medical college in Syracuse, New York, that would accept women."

"Did they accept her?"

"Yes. She was the second woman doctor in the United States and the first woman in America to receive a medical internship, just like men, at a hospital. She worked at Philadelphia Hospital just a few years ago."

"Thank you for telling me about her!"

"Sarah, don't let the lack of a physiology course stop you from pursuing your dreams. Like Sarah Adamson, you will have to find your own way—regardless of the obstacles you encounter."

"You're right. I won't give up. I promise. Where is Dr. Adamson now? Could I meet her?

"She lives in Rochester, New York, with her husband."

"Oh."

Mrs. Gillingham must have known what I was thinking, because she replied, "Yes, she got married, but she is still a doctor. She married a doctor and they work together. She is Dr. Sarah Dolley now."

So it is possible. I can't wait to tell Father. I could be a doctor and still be a wife.

"Do they have children?"

"Oh, yes. A little girl and a little boy—a lovely family."

"And she practices medicine—I mean for others, not just her family?"

"Absolutely. She is very well respected."

I hugged Mrs. Gillingham and ran out of the school. I couldn't wait to get home to tell Father and Mother what I had learned.

They listened to me as the words tumbled out of my mouth. I didn't ask for Friend Bones again. I figured telling them that Dr. Dolley's parents, good Quakers, got her a skeleton was enough said. All Mother said was, "That's nice, dear." Father did repeat her name twice though, as if not to forget it.

Maybe, just maybe.

Your friend,

Sarah

Goose Creek, Virginia

NINTH MONTH 7, 1858

Dearest Sarah,

A new school year has begun. This year, I will study much more difficult mathematics and computations. Maybe if Grandfather finds my calculations are improved, I will just help him with surveying roads, and we can forget his other business. I do want to be with Grandfather and help him, but with his mapmaking business and not anything else.

Mother wants me to go to school and go to meeting, pretending as if nothing is wrong. How can I do that when Grandfather's name and crime of abolition activity is published all over town? All I can think about is what everyone else must be thinking about the broadside.

At the Quaker meeting on First Day after the broadside was posted, no one spoke of the notice or its contents. Everyone acted as if all were well. Friend Samuel Sonns quite enthusiastically greeted Grandfather, almost as if he approved!

But I wonder. Have the slave catchers read the broadside? What about the sheriffs?

I was at Purcell's Store the other day and overheard some men talking about the loss of their "property" to the North. I knew immediately they were slave owners talking about their runaway slaves. They said conductors on the Underground Railroad have committed treason. One of the men mentioned Grandfather. He said that he should be arrested and tried for treason. "Of course we have to catch him in the act first. We'll get him. It's just a matter of time."

"That's not all," another man added. "We'll get those who help him. Anyone—anyone—who assists him in his abolitionist activities is as guilty as he is."

I froze. What can Mother and Father be thinking? Do they want me to get arrested too? Shouldn't they try to protect Grandfather, and encourage him to stop? It's simply too dangerous now.

I hid quietly behind the bolts of fabric and tried to hear what the men were saying. It sounded like they were planning something, but I couldn't make out the details. When they left the store, I quickly slipped out, kept my face hidden under my bonnet, and rushed toward home.

As I passed the meeting house, I was so deep in my own thoughts that I ran right into Joshua. "Hey, where are you going in such a rush?" he asked.

"I'm sorry. I guess I have a lot on my mind."

"Can I help?"

If only I could talk to Joshua about this. I am sure he has read the broadside. I wonder what he thinks.

Mother says that although Joshua has become a good friend to the family and a valued apprentice to Uncle Richard, he is not to know about the slaves staying at Evergreen. Well, I'm sure he knows now!

But all I could say was, "Thank you, Joshua, but I'm fine. Just a bit preoccupied right now. Will I see you at the wheat harvest?" Then without even waiting for his answer, I turned and walked quickly toward Evergreen.

Your friend,
Hannah

Philadelphia, Pennsylvania

NINTH MONTH 20, 1858

Dear Hannah,

I go to the Shelter several times a week now that school has begun. Most days, I work with Zebulon on his schoolwork and especially on his reading and writing. His wounds have healed very nicely. His spirit, though, is still in pain. He is cooperative, but withdrawn. I asked Mrs. Whitaker several times about his parents, but she has yet to tell me what happened to them.

Perhaps she thinks I am too delicate to hear the truth. If she only knew what I see in our home month in and month out. The details change, but the stories of cruelty are all the same. Israel escaped from Maryland and stayed in our home for two nights last week. He was obedient to his master, despite repeated whippings, because he had no choice. His wife and two-year-old boy were also owned by his master. The slave owner used the threat of selling Israel's wife and son just to keep Israel in his place.

But then one day, Israel came home from a long day in the fields to find that the master had sold his wife and his son to a plantation in Louisiana. He pleaded with his master to sell him too so they could stay together. His master would hear none of it, and gave him the worst whipping he ever had.

Several of the other slaves nursed him over the next few days as he was unconscious from the beating. When his wounds were healed enough that the scent of blood would not be on him, he put asafetida, a spice, on the soles of his shoes to throw off the hounds, and fled from the plantation.

The Committee plans to help him all the way to Canada. There he can work and perhaps earn enough money to purchase his wife and son. The problem is he doesn't even know who bought them. Father assured him that the Committee would try to discover that information and help Israel with his plan.

I learned there are some in our movement who travel in the South disguised as slave owners. They purchase slaves to set them on their way on the Underground Railroad. Often the slaves who are purchased are wives or children of those who have already escaped.

The southern planters have learned to raise the price substantially if they suspect such an attempt. A slave who would otherwise sell for $500 to $1,000 will often have a price of three times that much.

Dr. Dixon comes by the Shelter regularly and always asks for me to assist him, if I am there. Lately all I have helped with are sniffles, sore throats, and tummy aches.

It was good to see your grandfather again. He's working with Uncle Robert to publish his latest map. He says it has been quiet lately at Evergreen—no packages.

Your friend,

Sarah

Goose Creek, Virginia

NINTH MONTH 25, 1858

Dear Sarah,

The wheat harvest has begun, and frankly, I was relieved to be involved in something normal again. School is out for two weeks, as everyone is needed for harvesting the wheat crop.

Father is excited about this year's harvest. Not only has the weather been perfect this summer, but also the crop has come in strong and stands tall. There should be plenty for our needs and enough left over to sell or exchange.

On the second day of the wheat harvest, Joshua challenged the men to a contest. The winner had to cradle more wheat than any other man.

Mother smiled and said, "Joshua will have his hands full with Father in the match. No man cuts wheat as fast as your father." I felt torn. Of course I want Father to win, but then, it also would be good if Joshua won.

When we went to the fields at ten this morning to take the lunch, the men were in good spirits. The children carefully placed each man's shocks of wheat in a pile with his name. The women set up the boards and placed the ham, squash, carrots, and pies on the boards. We carried buckets of cool spring water for the men to drink. They were very appreciative but took only moments to eat their food and then hurried back to cutting the wheat. Each man was determined to win Joshua's challenge.

Mother and I watched the men work for a while. Mother leaned in and whispered to me, "Joshua is a strong man and a hard worker."

"Yes, Mother, and …?"

"And, I think he is trying to show off … for you!"

I blushed and told Mother that we better get the food into the shade and cover it up. I have to admit, though, it felt good to talk to Mother about something normal for a change.

The men did not stop their work until nightfall. The next morning they bound the cuttings into sheaves, and the children carried the sheaves to the threshing floor. The children stacked the sheaves in piles, again according to the man who had cut them.

At the end of the day, the men gathered to determine the winner. The total amount of harvested wheat came to 120 bushels! Word went out in the village and by nightfall many had come to see if it was true—yes, our men really had harvested 120 bushels of wheat.

There was much merriment among the men, and Father, who shocked the most wheat, teased Joshua, who came in second. "Age and experience sometimes win out over youth and enthusiasm."

Joshua laughed good-naturedly. "I will work hard all year to make sure I beat you next year."

I liked watching them laugh together. I went to bed happy but woke up with a start as I heard the clock strike eleven o'clock. There was something else too. I heard it. In the distance. Dogs. A pack of dogs. Slave patrols?

My heart pounded and I held my breath. Why are they so close? Is a slave coming to Evergreen? My candle was out, so I felt my way in the dark down the stairs and lit my candle stub from the embers in the fireplace. I peered out the window. I couldn't see anything, but the sound of the dogs was getting louder.

"Get away from the window." Grandfather's booming voice startled me.

I nearly dropped my candle. "You frightened me. Is it a slave? Is a slave coming to Evergreen?"

"Could be."

"Or it could be a trap. Grandfather, I heard some men talking in Purcell's Store about those who are helping the Underground Railroad. It sounded like they were planning something, but I couldn't hear what. I should have told you, but I guess I wanted it all to go away, so I just didn't want to think about it."

"It's all right. They've tried to stop me for years."

The sounds of the hounds grew louder. "Grandfather! They're coming down the road!"

"Snuff out thy candle!" He peered out the curtains, and listened hard. I saw that his ear trumpet was over on the table. I ran to get it for him and watched as he lifted it high and towards the window. He strained to hear.

Suddenly, my heart went out to Grandfather. I didn't realize how difficult it was for him. I whispered, "It sounds as though they are crossing onto our land now." I saw the anxiety flick across his face. He strained harder to hear. I asked, "What should I do?"

Grandfather whispered, "Stay low. Stay away from the windows. They will be here in just a few moments." I must have looked frightened because he added, "There are no fugitives at Evergreen right now."

The horses snorted as the men pulled up on the reins. The hounds barked like crazed animals, as if they had cornered their prey.

The men pounded on the door. "Open up, Taylor."

Grandfather held a finger to his lips. I wasn't about to say a word, but I was sure the men could hear my heart pounding. We moved quietly from the parlor to the hall where there were no windows. I bumped into a table and knocked over the candlestick. Grandfather grabbed it just seconds before it would have hit the ground.

"Taylor. We know you're in there. Open up."

Father crept silently down the stairs and put his hand on my shoulder. I mouthed, "Slave catchers!" Father nodded and kept his steadying hand on my shoulder.

"Scared to face us, Taylor? Take our property and hide in shame, is that what you're doing?" Grandfather clenched his fist and moved toward the door. He looked at me and stopped short. I could tell there was nothing more he'd rather do than open the door and face those men. It was all he could do to hold himself back.

The men rattled the door handle with the hounds baying loudly beside them. I held my breath. The doorknob twisted to the right. Was it locked? One push and they would be inside. I looked at Father in alarm. He pushed me behind him, stared at the door, and waited.

"Not man enough, eh, Taylor? This isn't over. We'll be back."

I heard the footsteps go down the porch steps. The men mounted their horses and galloped away, still cursing and shouting at Grandfather. We stood there for several minutes more before I could see Father relax. Grandfather lifted his ear trumpet and moved near the window. Satisfied that the men were gone, he let out a sigh.

"I am sorry they frightened thee, Hannah."

"Grandfather, this is what I mean. It's getting too dangerous now. For you. For all of us."

Father put his arm around me and pulled me close. I was still shaking.

Grandfather sat down and laid his ear trumpet at his feet. "Fear and intimidation is what they use to convince the slaves to stay in bondage, and fear and intimidation is what they use to try to convince us to run away from those who would seek our help. It will take a lot more than their scare tactics to stop me, though."

I had to wonder. If that is true, then what would these men try next?

Father told me to get back to bed. He and Grandfather would stay up to make sure they were gone. He said there was nothing to worry about anymore.

As I climbed the stairs, I shuddered. *Tonight perhaps, but what about tomorrow?*

> *Your friend,*
> *Hannah*

Philadelphia, Pennsylvania

TENTH MONTH 10, 1858

Dear Hannah,

There is much activity here. We have had one fugitive slave after another in our home. It seems as if the sounds of distant trumpets call them, urging them on, now more than ever.

My sewing circle meets three times a week now. The need for clothing is great. You can't imagine how tattered some of the runaways' clothing is, and they must dress warmly for Canada. I am so sorry that I've not been able to sew my square for the friendship quilt.

Lionel drove Zebulon and me out to Seven Oaks last weekend. Zebulon and Samuel picked pumpkins and helped William and Lionel load some of the fall harvest for the orphanage into the wagon.

When William came in with the boys for lunch, he agreed to watch Jonathan for a spell. Graceanna and I walked down to Roadside to visit Friend Lucretia Mott. We took some freshly baked bread with us. Friend Lucretia met us on the porch. She had just brought in her starching to iron. Graceanna insisted she let us help her, and soon we were sorting, ironing, and folding the freshly starched fabrics.

Friend Lucretia insisted we stay for lunch: corn soup, fresh bread, and apple slices.

After lunch, we took mugs of hot tea into the parlor. The fire crackled in the Franklin stove. By Friend Lucretia's rocking chair was a two-shelf table covered with papers and books. To her left was a basket of mending, and behind that basket was another filled with rags to make carpets.

She settled down with her mug of tea and said, "Tell me about thy service at the orphanage."

I told her about Zebulon. I told her everything I knew.

Graceanna shared about what she had seen in Zebulon's eyes as he played with Samuel.

Friend Lucretia closed her eyes and said, "Times to run free — to learn how to be free — are good for his soul. Thee should keep coming to Seven Oaks with Zebulon."

I told Friend Lucretia that I did not know what had happened to Zebulon's parents, but they weren't with him anymore. And that he never speaks about them.

"They are not far away from him in his thoughts, though," she answered.

"How do you know?" I asked.

"Look in his eyes. Thee will know it too."

I was confused. I try to look in his eyes, but he doesn't want me to. Friend Lucretia hasn't even met Zebulon. What does she know about his eyes?

As if guessing my silent questions, Friend Lucretia said, "The stories of slavery are all different, and yet they are all the same."

Graceanna explained, "Friend Lucretia and her husband have helped many a runaway escape to freedom."

Friend Lucretia sat forward. "Graceanna tells me thee wants to be a doctor."

"Oh, yes." I poured out my heart's desire, my frustration with my parents' reluctance, and the encouragement from Mrs. Gillingham.

"Dr. Dolley. Sarah Dolley. A friend indeed."

"You know her?"

"She and her husband provide a final stop on the Underground before Canada."

My mouth dropped open. Can you believe it? Dr. Dolley is a conductor on the Underground Railroad. I can't wait to tell Father and Mother.

We had to leave, but Friend Lucretia insisted I come back to visit the next time I was at Seven Oaks. She promised to have some eggs and scrapple from her farm for us to take back to the orphanage.

We walked quickly back to Seven Oaks as the sun was getting lower in the summer sky. We would have just enough time to get back to Philadelphia before dusk.

Zebulon and Samuel were proud of how hard they had worked to fill the wagon with food. It was stacked high with pumpkins, squash, late season corn, and beans. It took a few minutes for Zebulon to find a spot to nestle down among all the baskets of food. We waved good-bye as Lionel flicked the reins, and the horses began their plodding walk back to the city.

Zebulon fell asleep quickly, all tuckered out from playing with Samuel and helping to load the wagon. I sat up front with Lionel and enjoyed the afternoon sun on my face and the steady sounds of the hoof beats of the horses. I replayed my conversation with Friend Lucretia over and over in my mind. I imagined myself as a doctor. I even let myself think about being married. Suddenly, everything seemed possible.

When we were about halfway home, Lionel jarred me out of my daydreams. "Miss Sarah, I was wondering 'bout Zebulon. What happened to his parents? "I don't know," I answered truthfully.

"Where did the boy come from?"

"You know, I really don't know much about him. He'd already arrived at the orphanage when I started volunteering there."

I turned my face to the side of the road. I felt uncomfortable. Lionel had never talked to me about the children at the orphanage before. Why was he suddenly so interested in Zebulon?

Your friend,

Sarah

Goose Creek, Virginia

TENTH MONTH 13, 1858

Dear Sarah,

I have a solution! I know a way for us to correspond more often and work on our quilt at the same time. It came to me when I read your last letter. We can slip our letters inside a quilting square. It would appear to be ordinary needlework, but we can place our letters between the calico and the backing and slip stitch it closed. Then we will be able to write whenever we want and post them in the mail. And now you will have to work on our friendship quilt!

Grandfather and I took the buggy to Waterford today. We bought hominy, soap, and the drawing paper Grandfather needs for his maps.

It was good to see our friends at noonday. Grandfather and Friend Isaac Steer pulled their chairs close together in the parlor and kept their voices low. I wondered if Grandfather was telling him about the slave catchers.

Sarah Steer, Mollie Dutton, and her sister, Lida, arrived, and we sat out on the porch leaving Grandfather to his schemes. I had a grand time catching up on all the news of Waterford. Did you know Rebecca Russell is betrothed? She will marry in just a few months and move to Ohio.

On the way home Grandfather stopped in Leesburg. We visited Dr. Moore. Grandfather spoke with Dr. Moore for a long time while I studied his apothecary. I am so glad I have not been sick in more than a year, for if these medicines taste as horrid as they look, I should hate to take them.

I tried to imagine your being a doctor, dispensing medicines from your apothecary. Dr. Smith. Patients lined up outside your door. Friend Bones hanging up there in your office, frightening the children half to death!

Your friend,
Hannah

Philadelphia, Pennsylvania

Tenth Month 24, 1858

Dear Hannah,

You, my dear friend, are quite clever. Enclosed is my first square for our quilt. We will finish it yet!

The weather is still quite warm so we went to Seven Oaks yesterday. Zebulon bolted out of the wagon as soon as it slowed down. Samuel was waiting for him, and the two boys dashed off into the fields where William was working.

Lionel went to unhitch the wagon and water the horses. I greeted Graceanna and little Jonathan. Graceanna said that Friend Lucretia wanted to see me right away. She would stay with Jonathan.

When I arrived at Roadside, Friend Lucretia hurried me inside. "I need thy help today," she said.

"What can I do?" I asked.

She took me to the parlor where she was sorting newspapers. "I need to pass on the word to those who cannot afford such luxuries. If thee would sort these into bundles, I would be most glad. I keep the dailies for kindling, but the weeklies and monthlies should be sorted into eleven bundles." With that, she whisked herself out of the room, leaving me to stare at piles of newspapers several feet high.

I got to work. First I separated the dailies from the weeklies and monthlies. Then I sorted them by publisher. Finally, I sorted them by date. Most were anti-slavery newspapers, some were Friends publications, and others were city and town newspapers.

One headline in an anti-slavery newspaper caught my eye. MAN WEDS, THEN SELLS HIS WIFE. I sat down by the fire and read the article.

Though Philadelphia is a free state, its close proximity to the slave states creates a grave danger to those who would remain free. Kidnappers, paid by southern slave owners, are ever on the prowl to recapture runaways who have refuge in Philadelphia. They are paid handsomely for those they send south again.

Children play near the waterways with nary a worry as they are now free. Evil men lurk there ready to whisk them away, down the river, and back to the south for purchase, and the end of their freedom. The high price paid to kidnappers for a child, with all those years of toil ahead of them, makes them a valuable target.

Even with changed identities, new jobs, and new places to live, it is not safe in Philadelphia. Proslavery sentiment is rising. The Underground Railroad may have to go further underground to avoid detection and survive in the city of brotherly love.

If you are an escaped slave living in our city, watch for those who follow you and call you by your original name. They look for any sign of recognition or acknowledgement that you are the fugitive they seek.

Do not trust anyone. All is not what it seems. Slave catchers use decoys to lure out the fugitives and snatch them from their safe havens to spirit them to the south and enslavement again.

One man, enticed by the prize of a financial reward, believed he had located an escaped female slave from North Carolina now living in Philadelphia. Her description matched perfectly, but she now had the name of Patty Miller and worked as a laundress for a prominent Philadelphia family.

Although this man shared her race and enjoyed freedom himself, he stole her heart and then stole her life. He courted her for over a year, won her trust, married her, and then sold her back into slavery.

I put the newspaper down. I was stunned. I had no idea these things went on in Philadelphia. I will never take Zebulon to the river. I had no idea it was so dangerous.

Friend Lucretia came back into the room and I asked her about the article. She said, "These tactics have been used for many years, but recently, proslavery sentiment has been growing in Philadelphia. We must be careful, but we must not stop doing what we are doing."

I understand what you must be feeling, Hannah. I thought Philadelphia was safe. Have I endangered Zebulon by bringing him to Seven Oaks? No one knows he is here except William and Graceanna and the Motts. And Mrs. Whitaker and Lionel, of course. I must ask her what Zebulon's real name is. I'm sure she gave him a new identity.

Your friend,

Sarah

Philadelphia, Pennsylvania

TENTH MONTH 25, 1858

Dear Hannah,

Zebulon's real name is Zebulon. Mrs. Whitaker told me that she only changed his last name. She felt that he had been so traumatized by what had happened to his parents that she didn't want to add to his distress by changing his first name. What was she thinking? Zebulon is not that common a name!

I told Mrs. Whitaker what I had read in the newspaper. She told me not to worry and that Zebulon's identity is protected at the orphanage. Is it? Who else knows he is here? The Committee, of course. My parents. My brother's family. The slaves who were with Zebulon who were sent station to station all the way to Canada. Dr. Dixon. James, who delivers milk to us every Tuesday. Lionel, of course. And a score of volunteers.

"Have you made sure the volunteers are who they seem to be? I mean, Mrs. Whitaker, you really didn't ask me very many questions when I arrived to offer my services. What if I am a spy?"

Mrs. Whitaker laughed, and said, "Sarah, I know of your family and their reputation. You gave me your principal's name for a recommendation, remember? I made sure you were trustworthy before I put you in charge of these young lives. I do that for all the volunteers."

"What about Mr. Pennington?" I didn't like Peter Pennington, the peddler who came by every other week to sell his wares. Mrs. Whitaker sometimes bought candles, soap, or stationery from him.

"I don't like the way Peter Pennington scans the room every time he is here, as if he is looking for someone."

"Mr. Pennington has come by for over two years now to sell us his goods. The goods are always in fine shape, and he has never cheated me by one penny."

"But what do you know about him? I mean the newspaper said

this other man courted this woman for over a year, then he married her, before he turned on her."

"Sarah, you need to calm down. You are worried about Zebulon. I understand that. The article frightened you. I assure you Zebulon is safe. The orphanage is the best place for him right now. He will not be sold back to slavery. You have my word."

I hope that is true. I couldn't stand it if something happened to Zebulon.

Your friend,

Sarah

Goose Creek, Virginia

ELEVENTH MONTH 5, 1858

Dear Sarah,

It is cold enough to kill the hogs now. Rather nasty business that I prefer to stay out of, but Mother insists that this year I must learn to make hogshead cheese. Joshua came to help Father slaughter the hogs. They are preparing the hams for smoking in the smokehouse now. This is not the time to speak with Joshua. I prefer him with a surveyor's compass—rather than covered in hogs' blood.

We have not had a single visitor to Evergreen—no one knocking late at night needing a place to stay. Unless, of course, you count the slave catchers that pounded on our door.

Grandfather says it is because of the increase of patrols around our village since the posting of the broadside. Father says it is because this route is becoming too dangerous and more slaves are going westward over the mountains to the north. Mother says it is not time yet and that just as the land remains fallow before its most important crop, sometimes the home must rest before its most significant guest may arrive.

I think it is because I pray so very hard each night that no slave will find his way to Evergreen.

Always your friend,
Hannah

Philadelphia, Pennsylvania

ELEVENTH MONTH 30, 1858

Dear Hannah,

There is no more harvest to be gathered, but I convinced Mrs. Whitaker to let me take Zebulon for a visit anyway. I begged Lionel to take us even though he likes to be productive, and I knew there wasn't much left to do at the farm.

I knew Zebulon would love to be with Samuel. Truth be told, Zebulon is like a different boy for a few days after each visit to Seven Oaks. He still seems locked up inside, but when he is at Seven Oaks, he comes alive. I didn't want too much time to go by between visits.

I took my knitting with me. We are hard at work here preparing for the anti-slavery fair to be held the week before Christmas. This will be the largest bazaar ever, and we are determined to collect as many items as possible.

Aunt Alice has been working with me for a month on what are sure to be the most treasured items at the bazaar. Aunt Alice appreciates the finest of fabrics and has in her possession some of the most beautiful silk textiles I have ever seen. She gave me several of her beautiful dresses to cut up for sewing.

Together we have sewn six silk purses out of each of her dresses. We have sewn every stitch as perfectly as possible. The purses are made of light blue silk, lined with cream silk, with silk drawstrings. On the front of each purse, we stamped the fabric with a transfer print of an enslaved man in front of a slave shack, with a young child on one knee and another child in his arms. In the background is a church steeple and another slave plowing a field. I brought one of these purses to show Friend Lucretia.

I also brought her a copy of the advertisement Aunt Alice and I made to send out to our friends. We know many of them come to the fair to buy gifts, so we made sure the advertisement listed the fine stationery, paintings, jewelry, and embroidery for sale. Items from Europe will include Parisian notepaper stamped with initials, perfume, sandalwood fans, and statues. We should bring in more contributions this year than ever before.

When we arrived at Seven Oaks, William told Lionel that he had a surprise for him. A neighboring farm was going to send us home with seven turkeys for the children and one for Lionel. The hard work of slaughtering and dressing lay ahead for the men. Yuck. Lionel seemed glad he would not be just waiting around for me to return to the Shelter, and rolled up his sleeves and walked off with William.

Of course, the boys were off again in a split second of arrival. You could hear them laughing and hollering as they ran off. It is so good to see Zebulon like this.

Jonathan toddled after them, and Graceanna was not far behind him. She said I should go on to Roadside without her. "Jonathan is a handful today. As kind as Friend Lucretia is, I don't think I will inflict Jonathan on her today!"

When I got to Roadside, Friend Lucretia saw I had brought my knitting bag. She clapped her hands. "Oh, delightful. I was hoping we could knit together today."

We settled into the parlor, and she added a log to the fire. As the embers swelled into flames, we compared notes on items being donated or made for the anti-slavery fair. I showed her the purse I had made, and she murmured her approval. I pulled the advertisement out, and she brightened. "I do think this will be the best fair yet!"

I put away the purse in my kitting bag and pulled out my needles with my nearly complete project on them. I began to knit.

Friend Lucretia said sharply, "What is that yarn there?"

I had no idea what she meant. "This is yarn Mrs. Whitaker gave me to make a bureau cover for her to donate to the fair."

"Here, let me see it."

I handed over my knitting needle with my stitching attached. Friend Lucretia studied it, and then with one swift motion, pulled my handwork off the needle and tossed it in the fire.

"Southern cotton," she explained. "It won't do to have southern cotton in an article for sale at the anti-slavery fair, now will it?"

I was astonished. I had never even thought about where the yarn came from. It's just yarn.

"We cannot help the success of the plantations in any way. Southern cotton comes from the backs of the ones we are dedicated to free."

My face darkened. I realized where Mrs. Whitaker had gotten her yarn. Peter Pennington. I knew I didn't like that man. He buys southern cotton to sell to a woman who runs an orphanage for colored children, some of whom worked as slaves in the very fields that made that cotton.

"Now, start over. Use my yarn. It comes from London. I assure thee it is free cotton."

I selected from the vast array of colors she offered me from the balls of yarn in her basket and cast my stitches on my needle to begin again.

"Now, tell me about thy doctoring."

We spent the rest of the afternoon talking and knitting. It was all too soon time to return to the Shelter. Friend Lucretia sent me out the door with my knitting bag filled with English yarn made of free cotton, and a promise to come back soon.

I glanced in the back of the wagon. It was filled with eight plump birds, dressed and ready for the oven, in wood boxes filled with ice. Lionel whistled most of the way back. I complimented his work and told him the children would be thrilled. "Me too, Miss Sarah. The missus will be surprised at what I am bringing home tonight."

There was no room for Zebulon in the back with all those birds, so he rode up front with Lionel and me. The rhythmic swaying of the wagon and the pattern of the clip clop of horses' hooves soon had Zebulon falling fast asleep. I reached over and pulled him in tight under my arm. He didn't resist and curled up beside me. In less than a minute, he was asleep.

Your friend,

Sarah

Philadelphia, Pennsylvania

TWELFTH MONTH 18TH, 1858

Dearest Hannah,

Our fair these last three days was a glorious success. We raised much-needed funds for the anti-slavery movement—some $1,700 this year. We had wonderful speakers, including Robert Purvis and William Wells Brown. Friend Lucretia Mott spoke as well. She was spellbinding as always.

I'm sorry I haven't been able to work on our friendship quilt until now. Today I worked a nice square for you with some leftover silk from the purses we made.

Your friend,

Sarah

Goose Creek, Virginia

FIRST MONTH 19, 1859

Dear Sarah,

Last night after we had all gone off to bed, there was a steady, insistent knocking on the door. They did not know, but I was nearby. It was not like the sound of the pounding on the door of the slave patrols a few months back. This knocking was softer, more unsure.

Grandfather opened the door, with Father not far behind. A tall man stood framed by the light of Grandfather's candle. The man asked, "Does a Friend live here?"

Grandfather replied, "Indeed he does. Come in."

In stepped a man who by his appearance must have been a slave. He was muscular, but looked as though he had not eaten for days. His clothes were torn and nearly falling off him. His shirt was in shreds, and when he turned, I saw scars and massive welts upon his back and shoulders. He must have been beaten many times.

Grandfather clasped the hand of the tall, dark stranger and bid him come to the kitchen to eat. The man then turned to Grandfather and said, "I have my young'un with me. Had to make sure it was safe first."

"By all means, bring the child inside."

The man slipped out into the night. Moments later he returned with a frightened, half-frozen waif of a girl, who peeked out from behind him. "This here's Pearl," her father said.

Grandfather stooped down to look directly into her eyes and said, "Pearl, thee is safe here. Come and eat."

Mother cooked a grand breakfast—even though it was just after midnight. I nodded at Pearl and quickly got sheets to tack up over the windows. I didn't want any slave patrols that might come by to see that slaves had come to Evergreen.

When I was finished, I stared at Pearl. I don't know what I was

expecting when I met my first slave at Evergreen, but this wasn't it. I think Father thought I was being rude because he asked me to help Mother serve the food.

The man ate seven biscuits, six eggs, and more than a pound of our best bacon. At first Pearl just picked at her food. Finally her father told her, "Eat, child." Only then did she plow into the food on her plate. You would think these folks hadn't eaten in weeks.

After they ate, Mother brought out one of my favorite dresses and helped Pearl put it on. I think she must be about ten or eleven because my dress nearly swallowed her up. Then Mother asked Pearl if she wanted to rest, but Pearl was too frightened to leave her father's side.

The men moved to a corner of the room to talk. Mother tried to speak with Pearl, but she would say nothing. I think I now know what it's been like for you with Zebulon.

I was more interested in what Grandfather had to say, anyway. He told Pearl's father, who goes by the name of Joseph, that there was too much snow for him to cross the river. Passage likely could not be arranged for another four to six weeks. Grandfather told Joseph that he and Pearl were welcome to hide out at Evergreen until they could safely continue their journey.

Six weeks! Since I first learned about Grandfather's involvement, we have not had a single runaway slave arrive at Evergreen—not even for one night. And now we have two fugitives, staying for over a month? I couldn't believe what I was hearing.

Father motioned to Mother, who came near to him at the washing sink. I brought the plates over to the sink so I could hear too. Father told Mother that he was worried about being found out. People were watching Grandfather's every move. Hiding two slaves on the farm for six weeks in the dead of winter would be a challenge. We would have to hide them in the house.

This made me even more angry. Great! Two slaves. One wearing my favorite dress. Both eating our food and staying in our home for six long weeks while people are trying to catch Grandfather in the

act of helping slaves escape. How ever are we to make it through this?

Grandfather then motioned for Joseph and Pearl to follow him up to the third floor. He asked me to light a lamp for them and bring it up. He showed Joseph his special room, where he had his drafting table, a small bed, and a chair. Quilts were piled in one corner.

He showed them a little door under the eaves, where they were to hide if necessary. "If trouble comes," Grandfather explained, "we will put the chest over the door to hide it from view. Now thee must get some rest."

Joseph, with downcast eyes, said, "Thank you, Master Taylor."

At that Grandfather turned around with great ferocity — so much in fact that Joseph and Pearl began to shake. Even I trembled with surprise. "I am not thy master, Joseph. I am thy friend. In this house thee shall call me Friend Yardley Taylor. Friend Yardley. And look up, man — look me in the eyes. You are special to God and therefore to me."

We were all shaking. I had never heard Grandfather's voice boom like that. Pearl wouldn't dare lift her head, and her shoulders shook with fear. I didn't blame her. I'd be scared too.

Her father stood tall and shook Grandfather's extended hand. Joseph's hand was so large, it almost covered Grandfather's. "Thank you. Thank you, Mister Taylor, sir."

Grandfather then placed his other hand over Joseph's and said gently, "Yardley, sir. Friend Yardley."

I could hardly sleep at all that night. How could I, knowing that two slaves were sleeping in the room above me? Yet, I also could not get Grandfather's words out of my head. I must think more on this someday — once the slaves have left our home. Yes, then I will think about it.

The next morning, Grandfather told me the two had been running for months. They had left Oakwood Plantation on the Edisto River in South Carolina and stayed in forests and swamps, where they lived on berries and fish. Once it turned cold, they ran for weeks with only the North Star to guide them. Someone in Culpeper County told them that if they made it to Evergreen near the river, they could make it to freedom. In Winchester they overheard a man say he was going to the foundry at Evergreen in Goose Creek, and they knew that freedom was not far away.

The morning after that, Grandfather asked me to go to school as usual. I was torn. I didn't really want to be around Pearl and her father, but I guess I was curious and wanted to stay to learn more. Grandfather told me we would talk more tonight.

"Pearl's mother died right before they began to run. Thee must do thy part to make her feel welcome. Did you know she is about your age?"

I felt bad for Pearl. I can't imagine what she has been through the last few months. And I'm sorry that her mother died. I am. Truly. But I'm also angry that they are here, putting us in danger.

It's only been a few months since the broadside was posted naming Grandfather as some awful criminal who helps slaves escape. The patrols come by frequently with their baying hounds sounding a warning to us. I know they are watching. One slip up and Grandfather is going to be arrested!

Grandfather interrupted my thoughts. "Obey thy mother and father in whatever they ask. I will go to Philadelphia to consult certain Friends there about this special case. I've never had a child come through before."

Tonight I will ask him to deliver this letter to you in person. It must not fall into the wrong hands. Please write back so Grandfather can bring me your advice soon. I value your thoughts and wisdom, dear friend.

Anxiously I await your reply,

Hannah

Philadelphia, Pennsylvania

FIRST MONTH 25, 1859

Dear Hannah,

I have enclosed a clipping Father found in the Philadelphia newspaper. You must be very careful, Hannah.

$250 REWARD

> *Runaway from the Subscriber from Oakwood Plantation on the Edisto River, Dorchester County, South Carolina, on the night of 22nd September last, his Negro man Joseph, a man of full height, very erect, about forty years of age. He is well spoken and can tell a very plausible story. He is stoutly built, strong with large limbs, six feet two inches high, wearing a brown wool jacket and denim breeches. Accompanying the runaway is his daughter, Pearl, about age 14, a bright and smart-looking child. It is supposed they are making their way north and that they will travel chiefly at night. The above reward will be paid upon return to me or to any jail in South Carolina.*

Buck Worthy, Charleston, S.C.

I know you are frightened and confused, but might it not be that the Lord has placed you in this place at this time for this very reason?

Your friend,

Sarah

Goose Creek, Virginia

FIRST MONTH 30, 1859

Dear Sarah,

I could not believe my eyes when I saw the advertisement in the newspaper you sent. Father says the advertisement also ran in the newspaper here. What will we do?

I heard the patrols again last night. The dogs yelped and barked as if they had cornered a possum. I couldn't sleep one bit knowing who was upstairs. I hope Grandfather returns to Evergreen soon with a plan. I hope the plan will be for Joseph and Pearl to move on very quickly now. After all, with the advertisements and the dogs, they should not stay with us a day longer. That is my opinion.

Mother doesn't agree. She notes that Pearl needs nourishment. Mother says Pearl is weak from too many cold nights and not enough food. Pearl looks just fine to me. Mother does not believe she could survive a journey across the Catoctin Mountains in this cold weather. Father is concerned as well and talked with Mother about the secret room under the barn floor. Because of the cold, he does not want them to stay there unless absolutely necessary. But I can tell even Father is worried about the frequency of the dog patrols around Evergreen.

I am trying to be brave but it is difficult. Grandfather has drawn too much attention to us in the past few years by speaking out against slavery. The dangers are great. The penalties are severe. If Grandfather gets arrested this time, it is unlikely he will escape a sentence as before. The temper of the times is changing here in Virginia. Some say only bloodshed and war will solve the question of liberty for slaves.

Joshua stopped by today. Mother greeted him warmly, but I was horrified. He needed to leave quickly before he suspected anything was wrong.

"I've got some mathematical equations for you to work. Master these and you will be much needed in our surveying."

He started to spread out the papers on the table as if we were going to sit down and go over them together. That is the last thing I needed. I scooped up the papers and said, "I'm so sorry. I can't work on them now. Let's do it later." I shoved the papers back into Joshua's hands and edged him towards the door. "Let's meet over at Uncle Richard's tomorrow. I'll bring a pie. We can work on them then."

The idea of a slice of warm pie seemed to do the trick. Joshua left, saying he'd see me after school tomorrow.

I don't know where Joshua stands on this issue of aiding fugitive slaves. He's never spoken about this. I wonder why. I mean, he never once brought up the broadside, and he knows it named Grandfather. Maybe he silently agrees with what the broadside said.

What if Joshua found out about the slaves hiding at Evergreen — what would he do? Would he betray us? To an orphan a $250 reward might be *very* tempting.

I am deeply troubled in my spirit, Sarah. Please pray for me.

Your friend,
Hannah

Goose Creek, Virginia

SECOND MONTH 1, 1859

Dear Sarah,

Thank you for your letters hidden in the pot Grandfather brought back from Philadelphia. He also brought back news of the Committee and what they think we should do.

Late at night, Grandfather asked me to tack up sheets on the windows again. He brought Joseph and Pearl down from the third floor to talk about the plan. They sat around the table with the one lamp light kept very low. I prepared mugs of hot cider for everyone, but mostly I wanted to hear firsthand what Grandfather found out in Philadelphia.

Grandfather showed Joseph the advertisement. Neither Joseph nor Pearl could read, but Joseph recognized that it was an ad for their capture. Grandfather read the advertisement to them. At the mention of Buck Worthy's name, Joseph grew cold.

Grandfather noticed. "Joseph, tell me more about the planter. My sources in Philadelphia said he is a successful planter near the barrier islands of South Carolina. I understand that Oakwood Plantation is known for its superior long-staple cotton."

"That is true," Joseph began. "And Master Worthy set his daughter in the kitchen to play. The house servants watched over her. They didn't know that this young'un told her daddy everything she heard them say." He hesitated. "One day while they was shelling peas for supper, they said I was sweet on a slave girl on a plantation downriver." He stopped for a minute and whispered, "Charity." Then he broke out in a huge smile. "She was the prettiest thing you ever laid eyes on. Met her when I did business for Master Worthy at her plantation."

"Then what happened?" Grandfather asked.

"Master got 130 field slaves. He put me in charge of them to keep them in their place. Did it like I wanted to — not like Master does. No whippings from me. Other slaves said they worked for me, not for Master. Cotton grew long and strong. Master thought, 'Hmm … can't lose my overseer. Don't want him to run away 'cause he makes my cotton grow and that makes me money.'"

"Yes, I understand," Grandfather said.

"Master smart. He learned 'bout Charity, and that was that. Master bought her in a snap. Master rode out to the fields, called me aside, and said, 'I bought Charity today.' The look in my eyes told Master everything he needed to know. He had just bought my loyalty."

I frowned. "I don't understand. Didn't the plantation owner do a good thing by buying Charity for Joseph?"

"Well," said Grandfather, "certainly Joseph and Charity were glad to be together, but they could not rest in the union. If Master Worthy could bring them together, then Master Worthy could tear them apart. He owned them both. He could sell one or the other at a moment's notice."

"That's right," said Joseph. "And Master knew he had me. So long as I was with Charity, then I wouldn't run away. It worked too. Master even let me and Charity get married."

Grandfather explained that a slave marriage is not legal in South Carolina, but Master Worthy permitted Joseph and Charity to marry.

"The way I sees it is that you gotta work as hard as the next man, and they will work for you."

Pearl chimed in, "Daddy worked as hard and as fast as any of the field slaves. If he got a bit of meat from hunting, then Daddy made sure he shared it with a slave beaten by the master."

"So, Master Worthy start to trust me, you know? He'd let me take the wagon into Georgetown.

Got me a special tag so if I got stopped, the white man would know it was okay for me to be on the road with Master's wagon." He nodded grimly. "I bided my time. Charity and me, we had a family."

Pearl said, "I have an older brother, William, and a younger sister, Talitha."

"Where are they?" I asked.

"I'll get to that part," said Joseph, "but I want to tell you about Charity first. Oh, how that woman loved Jesus. She would spend hours praying for her children. From the time they was little, Charity would sing songs about the love of Jesus. She wanted to get the truth of the songs into the hearts of her children."

"She sounds wonderful," I said.

"Yes, but a few years ago William told his mama that Christian teaching was just a southern way to keep slaves in their place. He began to talk about running away. We begged him not to cause trouble for our family. William said that was just what Master Worthy wanted. William tried to run away three times. Each time he was caught and beaten bad, the last time, almost to death. Just 'bout broke his mama's heart."

I thought it looked like it had broken Joseph's heart too. It was a minute before he could go on.

"Then one day, Master called me to his study and told me that he had decided to sell William to a plantation in Alabama. I begged him not to. I told him I'd get some sense into him. Master said, 'That boy is as bad for my plantation as you are good for it. He's got to go.'"

"Charity was pregnant with our fourth child at the time. That summer Charity became very ill with swamp fever that ravaged the plantation, and she died. The baby died with her."

"And your other child?" asked Mother.

"Ah," said Joseph. "Talitha. She only six now. After Master sold William and Charity died, Master thought I might not have a reason to stay around no more. He right too. I was just waiting for the right time to escape."

"What did he do?" I burst out.

"Master took Talitha into his home and gave her to his wife. Talitha's job was to stay up all night by the cradle of their little girl, Angelina. If the baby girl awoke, she was to rock her back to sleep so as not to disturb the slumber of the master and his wife. She was always under the Worthys' watchful eyes—in the master and mistress' bedchamber each night, tied to the bed, and as a house servant each day."

I looked at Pearl. She was whispering something. Sounded like Bookie. I could tell she misses her sister a great deal.

Father added, "This plantation owner, Buck Worthy, believed that if he kept Talitha, then somehow he would have a hold on Joseph. After all, how could he leave the last child he had with his beloved wife?"

"That's right, sir. Wasn't gonna leave my littlest girl."

"But you did," I said simply. "What happened? I know you didn't want to leave her."

"Had no choice. Had to get Pearl outta there. Get to Canada and Freedom Land. Then I'm gonna go back and get Talitha."

Grandfather said, "Buck Worthy is well known to some on the Committee. He prides himself on never having a runaway slave who does not return—dead or alive. He hires slave catchers to go after runaways, and he likely has one on their trail now."

I felt my blood run cold. Mother took one look at my face, and said it was time for me to go to bed. For a long time I sat by the window looking out over the garden. I could not go to sleep. Not while Pearl and her father slept above my room. I could not stop imagining the sounds of dogs on their trail, men with guns, and little Talitha crying out for her family and no one there to comfort her.

I remembered what Joshua had told me about orphans. I opened my Bible and found the place where God promises to care for orphans. "Lord," I prayed, "you promised that when a father and mother are not there to care for their children, you will watch over them. Watch over little Talitha tonight. Keep her safe."

Sarah, I am still afraid and unsure. I guess I do want them to move on as soon as possible. Yet up until now this Railroad business did not have faces or names—names like Pearl or Joseph or little Talitha.

Your friend,
Hannah

Goose Creek, Virginia

SECOND MONTH 2, 1859

Dear Sarah,

Mother prepared a basket with bread, ham, milk, and dried peaches. She's quite concerned about Pearl's appetite. Pearl hardly weighs a thing and eats next to nothing. Mother told me this morning that she does not think Pearl is quite right.

Well, Mother was right. I took the basket up to the third floor. When I saw Pearl, even I knew there was something very wrong. I ran to get Mother.

Mother felt her forehead. Pearl was blistering hot to the touch. Mother had me get cold water and cloths to bathe her forehead to get her fever down. Pearl could not seem to swallow even a sip of water.

I ran out to the creek and chipped slivers of ice into a bowl. Her fever was so high that when I would slip an ice chip into her mouth, it seemed to melt straightaway. Joseph wrung his cap and paced the room.

When the ice chips ran out, I ran downstairs and flung on my cloak to go get some more ice. Grandfather saddled Frank and rode off to Doctor Janney's place. I told Father that Grandfather shouldn't take those kinds of chances. "We should nurse Pearl ourselves."

"You must trust me. Doctor Janney will not divulge our secret."

When Grandfather returned, he did not have Doctor Janney with him. He said that for the sake of precaution, he came first. Doctor Janney would come along shortly, as if paying his good friends a friendly, not a medical, visit.

When Doctor Janney finally came, I led him up to see Pearl. Doctor Janney looked concerned as he examined Pearl.

I came back down with him after his examination. "Pearl is very ill. She should not be moved, and great care should be given

to get some liquids into her." He turned to Mother and me. "You are giving her excellent care. I want you to use mustard plasters, and prepare this medicine according to the directions." He handed it to Mother, and I looked over her shoulder. The recipe called for a tablespoon of salt, the juice of a lemon, and castor oil. "Twice a day. And have her drink as much snakeroot tea as she will tolerate. I'll be back in a few days to check on her."

She's not supposed to be moved. I wonder how long it will be before she is well enough to travel?

Your friend,
Hannah

Philadelphia, Pennsylvania

SECOND MONTH 3, 1859

Dear Hannah,

A visitor came by last night and told Mother and Father that they should expect two packages from Virginia to arrive in a fortnight. I wish you could come too. I understand your grandfather will deliver the packages to us. We'll be waiting.

Your friend,

Sarah

Goose Creek, Virginia

SECOND MONTH 5, 1859

Dear Sarah,

Today Pearl was much worse. Mother and I took turns nursing her. I tried to get her to drink a little snakeroot tea, but she would only take the ice chips again. Mother sang to her, and I saw Pearl curl up a little closer to Mother as she wiped her fevered brow. I could not help but think about how blessed I am to have a loving mother.

Appreciatively,
Hannah

Goose Creek, Virginia

SECOND MONTH 10, 1859

Dear Sarah,

Finally Pearl's fever has broken. Doctor Janney came by today and said she's beyond danger, which gave Joseph much needed relief. When Doctor Janney heard Grandfather's plan for the next part of their journey, he said Pearl needs about two months' rest before she would be ready to make such a long and perilous journey to Canada. He said that she should not travel before spring.

Spring! That is much too long. Someone is bound to find out she's hiding here. Grandfather and Father spoke in hushed tones all morning.

Do you know what else Doctor Janney told us? A man from South Carolina named Robert Blockett has been asking at doctors' offices in Leesburg whether anyone has treated a tall Negro man or a teenage Negro girl who could be runaway slaves. Grandfather said that he's a slave catcher. And Doctor Janney nodded. A slave catcher! Right here in our county, just miles from Evergreen. What if he comes to our home?

Your friend,
Hannah

Philadelphia, Pennsylvania

SECOND MONTH 15, 1859

Dear Hannah,

Nathaniel came by again today to invite me to go ice skating on the Schuylkill River. Mother insisted that I go and nearly pushed me out the door. "Have fun!" she called out after us. It was pretty obvious.

We met a bunch of others from Friends Central and skated for hours. I have to admit that I had a wonderful time. Nathaniel is a great skater, and I enjoyed being with him. Lydia was there, but he didn't even look her way.

Later, when Nathaniel walked me home, I invited him in for hot cocoa. Father was meeting with someone from the Committee. I overheard Father mention some packages from Virginia before he closed the door to his study. I was dying to know what they had decided about Joseph and Pearl. I rushed Nathaniel through his drink, thanked him for the good time, and showed him the door. He looked puzzled.

I felt guilty, so I called out as he walked down the street, "It was fun. Let's do it again." Nathaniel didn't turn around, but waved to let me know he heard me.

I rushed back inside and knocked quietly on the study door. Father opened it and let me come in. "Is there a plan yet?" I asked. "For Joseph and Pearl?" The Committee member nodded to Father and said he would let himself out.

Father explained, "We need to get Joseph to Philadelphia immediately. It's much too dangerous to keep him at Evergreen any longer. He is Buck Worthy's most valuable slave, and there is a steep price on his head. He's wanted back alive, not dead, which makes it harder for the slave catchers. Buck Worthy knows this and has increased the reward." He paused. "Joseph will stay with us for one night here in Philadelphia."

"And after that?" I asked.

"We won't know where he goes next. It's better that way. He'll continue on all the way to Canada."

"And Pearl?"

"Pearl will stay behind, for now. She's not strong enough to travel, and the Committee needs more time to plan her escape. They hope that with the slave catchers on the trail of Joseph, thinking that Pearl is with him, then that will throw them off the trail of Pearl."

I'm glad I will soon meet Joseph. I feel like I know him already from your letters.

I know Pearl will be worried after her father leaves. She'll have no one but you and your family once her father is gone. Try not to be afraid for yourself, but put yourself in Pearl's shoes.

Speaking of shoes, we are collecting as many pairs of good shoes as we can. So many of the packages delivered to us do not have shoes. From here on out, it is a cold journey without a good pair of shoes that can take the snow and ice.

Your friend,

Sarah

Philadelphia, Pennsylvania

SECOND MONTH 16, 1859

Dear Hannah,

After school, I went to the Shelter. Zebulon was very quiet. It's been a long time since we've been to Seven Oaks. I worked with him on his writing and although he was cooperative, he wasn't the same Zebulon I see in Cheltenham. I tried everything. Silly jokes. Funny faces. Nothing would make him laugh. Finally, he moved away and stared out the window.

Lionel dropped a load of kindling by the fire. He saw me watching Zebulon. "Been like that for weeks. Can't get him to talk."

I went into Mrs. Whitaker's office and sat down. "I don't know how to reach him. It seems like he is warming up to me, and then he shuts down again."

"It will take time. Just keep doing what you are doing. He'll come around."

I was just about to ask her about Zebulon's parents when who should burst into her office but Peter Pennington.

"Good day, Ma'am. And you too, Miss Smith. I have lots of special items for you today." He set his suitcase up on Mrs. Whitaker's desk and opened it.

"Like yarn made with southern cotton?" I asked.

Mr. Pennington looked up in surprise.

"I guess you thought we'd never find out, didn't you?" I stared at him. He seemed uncomfortable but didn't flinch.

"Mrs. Whitaker, this man sold you cotton made on the plantations. Remember the yarn you gave me to knit your donation for the fair? Well, Friend Lucretia confirmed it—southern cotton."

"Mr. Pennington?" Mrs. Whitaker asked. "You know we are Quakers."

Mr. Pennington seemed flustered, but quickly composed himself. "I got it in a trade. I had no idea. Why, I would never offend you like that."

My eyes narrowed. He's lying. And Mrs. Whitaker is believing him.

"Who'd you trade with? The plantation owner?"

"No, a woman in Camden, New Jersey. She had ten baskets of the yarn and gave me a really good deal."

"Well, well," said Mrs. Whitaker, wanting to change the subject, "what have you brought us today?"

I stormed out of there. I do not like Peter Pennington. I know he is lying. I don't trust him. I don't know why Mrs. Whitaker does.

Your friend,

Sarah

Goose Creek, Virginia

SECOND MONTH 20, 1859

Dear Sarah,

I woke this morning and Grandfather was gone. So was Joseph. Grandfather is taking Joseph across the Catoctin Mountains—a difficult journey for any man and much too difficult for Pearl. I asked Father why he didn't go in Grandfather's place. Father shook his head. "I tried, but you know your grandfather." Yes, I do. He wouldn't want anyone else to risk capture.

"Did he take Frank?"

"Yes, he did. That is some solace." I agreed. Frank is a sure-footed steed and Grandfather's most trusted companion in these situations.

Grandfather left me a note:

Dearest Hannah,

Do not fear. Be strong. Thy help is now needed. Thee must care for our special guest as I would. Obey your parents. Love your enemy.

Thy grandfather

Father told me that Uncle Oliver will tell others that Grandfather has taken off on another of his nursery expeditions. Uncle Oliver learned of a new variety of Ginko tree that arrives in Philadelphia soon by ship. Everyone knows how excited Grandfather gets when a new species of tree or plant comes to America. No one will be suspicious of his absence. Uncle Richard will take over the United States mail route until Grandfather returns. It may be weeks.

After I read Grandfather's note, Mother asked me to take Pearl her breakfast. I also gave her a message from her father, who had slipped away while Pearl was sleeping.

Pearl jumped a foot high off the bed when I opened the door. Her eyes darted around the room in fear. I put down the basket of bread and fruit, folded my arms across my chest, and said, "Your father left in the middle of the night with my grandfather. He said to tell you that he will see you in Freedom Land—at the end of the Liberty Line."

Sarah, we both just stood there staring at each other. Neither of us knew what to do. Finally I turned and left the room, taking her chamber pot with me to empty. That Pearl is one strange girl.

When I came back inside, Mother explained that Pearl will be my special charge until she is strong enough to make the trip north herself. She told me I am to do all I can to prepare her for a life of freedom and for the challenges ahead. How am I supposed to do that? She won't even talk.

I am tired and I miss Grandfather. Oh, how I wish things were back the way they were.

Your friend,
Hannah

Goose Creek, Virginia

SECOND MONTH 24, 1859

Dear Sarah,

You will think me frightful. I could not stand it a moment longer. This scared young slip of a girl won't talk. Day in and day out I take her food. I empty her chamber pot. I talk to her. I ask her if she needs anything. She says nothing. I ask about her health. She does not respond. She is a sullen, unthankful girl, and after all my family is doing to help her and her father.

Today when I took her breakfast to her, she once again refused to say one word. I had to get her to talk.

"So, who is Bookie?"

Her eyes got wide and she cocked her head to one side.

"Remember the night you first came here? You told me about your sister. I thought I heard you say 'Bookie.' I was wondering who that is."

Pearl turned from me, but I saw tears in her eyes. Well, at least I was getting a reaction from her.

"Is it someone you knew? Someone from Oakwood Plantation?"

Pearl turned around slowly, stared at me a minute, and then whispered, "Her name ... is Tookie."

I was so excited, I almost danced a little jig right there. Pearl had finally spoken!

"Tookie. That's a great name. Is that what you call your sister?"

She nodded her head.

"I thought your father said her name was Talitha."

"Talitha is her given name. Tookie is my name for her. Talitha is from the Bible."

"What does Talitha mean?" I asked.

Pearl shrugged. "Don't rightly know. Mama picked it." Tears ran down Pearl's face. "Got to find a way to get Tookie out of there. Master Worthy ain't never gonna let her go. She watches Master's girl-child all night long. Why, Tookie is just a girl-child herself!

Master ties her to the cradle and to a bell. If Tookie lays down and tries to sleep at night, the bell rings. Then Master whips her. If the baby cries, Tookie has to rock her back and forth till she falls asleep again."

I asked, "Do you think Master Worthy would sell Tookie?"

Pearl said, "No, don't think he aim to do that. He want power over Pappy. He want Pappy to try to come back and get Tookie. Then he gonna get Pappy."

"Do you think your father would do that? Get to freedom and then turn around and go back to the slave country for Tookie?"

"I know he gonna do that. That's what he told me every day in the swamp. First he was gonna get me to freedom, then he was gonna come back to get Tookie."

"Pearl, that's too dangerous. He'll get caught."

"I know, Miss Hannah. But I don't think Pappy can live with hisself, knowing Tookie still with Master Worthy and he be in freedom."

Then she lowered her head and said very quietly, "Miss Hannah, do you think Pappy will come back for me?"

I realized that Pearl didn't understand the plan for her to join her father in Canada. She was probably still too weak from her illness to take it all in.

I explained about the Committee and told her all about you, Sarah. I said that one day soon, when she was strong enough, Grandfather would make sure she got to your home in Philadelphia. I told her about you and your parents and what you do with packages when they arrive.

I told her about Canada. I am so glad you told me so much about the settlements in Canada. I told her there are many, many American slaves living free lives in Canada and that she should not be afraid.

Then do you know what she said? Pearl said, "If I could just be brave like you, Miss Hannah."

Brave like me? I'm jelly on the inside. You would have been

proud of me. I told Pearl that she must be brave and strong because it is the only way she can help Tookie. Pearl seemed satisfied and began to eat her breakfast. Sarah, we have to make a plan. We have to help Tookie come north to join her father and her sister. Please ask your parents what we can do.

Your friend,
Hannah

Philadelphia, Pennsylvania

THIRD MONTH 4, 1859

Dear Hannah,

There is much excitement here as we wait for your grandfather and his companion. We expect them any day now. Father has met several times with the Committee to plan the next part of his journey and to plan for Pearl's journey as well. The plans for helping a girl traveling alone are quite tricky, and they are taking extra special care to think this through. Hannah, I think I am going to like Pearl.

I shared your letter about Talitha with my parents. Father said this would be a challenge, but one he is eager to take on. Do you remember how I told you there are some who travel in the South posing as slave owners? They try to purchase slaves who are relatives of those that have already made it to freedom. Perhaps this is how we can rescue Tookie. I mentioned it to Father, and he is going to talk to the others about it.

Mother said it may require a fund. She has some ideas for how we can raise the money. I do wish you would come soon so we can work on this together. However, I understand that you are needed there.

You must help Pearl get ready. Father told me that the Committee will have to be extra careful in arranging passage for her. A slave catcher hired by Master Worthy may be thrown off the trail because he is looking for a father and daughter traveling together. Yet soon he will realize they have separated. A girl traveling alone is much more suspicious. It will take great planning to make sure Pearl joins her father in Canada.

Now, did you notice that this is the ninth square I have sent to you? Perhaps we will finish this quilt after all.

Your friend,

Sarah

Goose Creek, Virginia

THIRD MONTH 8, 1859

Dear Sarah,

Things are going much better with Pearl now that she's talking.

"Miss Hannah. You call your hogs funny. You got to do it right."

"And what, pray tell, is the right way to call a hog?"

"Like this." She cupped her hands around her mouth and hollered, "Souie, souie. Sook, sook."

"Hush, Pearl, you want that slave catcher Blockett to hear you?"

"Well, if he's coming, so are the hogs. They'll chase him down."

We fell on the bed. I laughed so hard, I cried.

"Miss Hannah, there was a boy named Joel who was sweet on me. Every day he followed me to the pigpen just to try to talk to me. But he never could seem to get up his nerve. Just follow me out to the pig pen, then follow me back. Day after day."

"He said nothing?"

"Nothing! So finally I says to him, 'Mister, you follow me morning and night to this pigpen. Do you happen to be in love with one of these pigs? If so, I'd like to know which one it is, so I can tell that pig about your affections.'"

Pearl and I laughed until we thought our sides would split.

Later I asked her questions about her life at Oakwood Plantation. I didn't know if that would upset her, but she seemed eager to share about her life.

"Where did you live?"

"We lived in a cabin. I slept on a mattress Mama made from ticking. It was filled with cornhusks." I tried to imagine what that must feel like. It did not sound one bit comfortable to me, but Pearl didn't seem to mind.

"We got a ration of food from the master each week. 'Tweren't much, but we made do 'cause Pappy caught rabbits and possums that

Mama cooked. Mama tended a garden in the spring and summer. We worked the garden at night because it was cotton we tended by day."

The slaves were not allowed to stop work for any reason unless it was the Sabbath or Christmas Day. Why, if a slave died, Pearl said they had to have the funeral at night!

I was curious what the plantation owner let them do for their Sabbath. Pearl explained, "On the Sabbath, Mistress Worthy made sure all the slave children had a sort of Sunday school. They taught us Bible scriptures—not to read, mind you, as that was against the law. I tried to memorize them as best I could."

Pearl is really bright. She just needs someone to help her. She quoted the entire text of Psalm 23 to me just as it is in the Bible. Think what she could do if she learned to read and write.

"But the white folks service was 'cause we had to go. It was later in the day on Sunday that we really worshiped. We'd gather at the creek for singing, preaching, and praising. We not so quiet as the white folks. We dance, lift our hands to heaven, clap and sing."

"Quakers don't sing," I said. "And we sure don't dance—in church or out."

Pearl looked at me in shock. "They don't? Then how do they show God they is happy?"

She had a point there. I find my heart strangely warmed to this idea of body, mind, and spirit all worshiping together at the same time.

"Pearl, how old are you?"

"I don't rightly know. I imagine about fourteen, but I don't know for sure."

"Do you know what month and day you were born?"

"No. Don't know that either."

She brightened. "I know this though. If I was sold, I would fetch $1,000!"

Seems to me that is not the right number for her to know. Will that be how much we will have to raise to buy Tookie, I wonder?

Your friend,
Hannah

Philadelphia, Pennsylvania

THIRD MONTH 9, 1859

Dear Hannah,

I was discouraged today when I went to the Shelter. I read to Zebulon, but he seemed distracted. He did not want to work on any schoolwork. He seemed listless and sad. When it came time to say good-bye, he barely waved to me.

I went into Mrs. Whitaker's office. "We have to do something about Zebulon."

"Do you think you can arrange a trip to Seven Oaks soon?"

I brightened. "That is exactly what I will do. If anything should help, that is it."

When I got home, your grandfather had arrived with Joseph. They had traveled up the mountain range through western Pennsylvania rather than the regular way. Your grandfather said he had to be especially careful with that slave catcher on his heels.

Father said he's heard that Mister Blockett takes pride in his ability to return property alive to the masters of the southern plantations. And he is paid quite well for his efforts.

Joseph stayed with us for only one night. It was too dangerous for him to stay longer, because of the connection between our two families. I am glad I got to meet him. He was relieved to learn Pearl is feeling better and getting stronger. He said to tell Pearl he will never be happy until she's with him again in Freedom Land.

I'll write again as soon as I have some more news. Tomorrow Mother and I meet with our sewing circle to make more clothes. Joseph left with two new shirts I stitched myself, a pair of sturdy shoes that can stand this winter cold, a coat, and two pairs of pants. He has begun his journey. All I know is they are sending him from farm to farm. All else is secret. The Committee will let us know when he reaches Canada.

Your friend,
Sarah

Philadelphia, Pennsylvania

THIRD MONTH 10, 1859

Dear Hannah,

Your grandfather is on his way home to you with the letters I wrote while he was here. This letter will go by regular post inside my tenth square. We may finish our friendship quilt by fall.

Father told me last night that the Committee agrees an attempt to purchase Tookie from Master Worthy is a good plan, if we can raise the funds. They cautioned that Mister Worthy may see her as a way to entice Joseph back to his plantation, and he may refuse to sell her.

Yesterday I took Zebulon to Seven Oaks. Lionel was more than willing to go along. There's no produce to bring back, but Lionel brought his ax to split some wood.

It's been a few months since Zebulon and Samuel have been together. It always boosts Zebulon's spirits to be with Samuel, but not this time. Samuel tried to get Zebulon to come sledding with some other children, but he wouldn't.

"Zebulon, don't you want to go with Samuel?" I asked.

"No, Miss Sarah. I'll just stay here with you."

"Have you ever been sledding before?" I knew he hadn't as this was the first year he'd seen snow. Zebulon just stood there silently.

"What if I come with you?" I offered.

He leaned into me and twisted his foot back and forth on the floor. He looked at me, just for a brief moment, then pulled away.

"What about a book? Would you like me to read you a story? You can sit with me or by the fire, if you like."

Samuel tugged on Zebulon, not understanding why he wouldn't want to go outside to play. Finally he gave up, put his mittens on, and dashed outside.

That's how the entire afternoon went. I'd try to think of everything I could to draw Zebulon out of his shell. Zebulon seemed to come close, then he'd pull away.

When we got back to the Shelter, Lionel unloaded the wood from the wagon and stacked it by the fireplaces.

I shared with Mrs. Whitaker about Zebulon and how he didn't want to play with Samuel.

Mrs. Whitaker sighed and said, "Sarah, I'm going to share with you some hard things. Maybe what I share will help you reach Zebulon. I too am worried about him. He is not eating very much. He seems to be drifting further away from us." She gripped her hands together in her lap. "You remember that I told you Zebulon escaped with a group of slaves from an Alabama plantation? Well, I didn't tell you that his parents were in that group of runaways too."

Mrs. Whitaker said the overseer and his men pursued them with a pack of hounds. The slaves decided to split up to confuse the dogs. They promised to meet again on the other side of the river. Zebulon was with his parents and one other man.

This escaped slave said Zebulon was slowing them down and they were all going to get caught. Zebulon couldn't keep up with the adults. Zebulon's father carried him most of the way, but it did slow them down. The others reached the river before they did.

The next day, they could tell the hounds were not far behind. The other man was terrified, and told Zebulon, "You gonna get us killed, boy. You're too slow." He turned to Zebulon's father, and said, "You shoulda left him behind. He's nothing but trouble to us now."

According to Mrs. Whitaker, Zebulon's mother put her hand on Zebulon's head to reassure him, but he could see the fear in her eyes as well. Zebulon's father asked this man to make sure Zebulon caught up with the others. They were near enough to the river at that point.

"What you gonna do?" the man asked.

"We'll turn ourselves in, distract them; you just get Zebulon to the river, promise me?"

The man agreed, but Zebulon cried out, "No!"

"There's no time now, Zebulon," his father said. "Be brave. We'll come after you soon enough."

With Zebulon whimpering, the man took off running, but too soon the hounds caught up to where Zebulon's parents were. The man stopped and hid in the bushes to wait and see what would happen. If he kept going, there was too much chance that the hounds would follow him. If the men returned to the plantation with Zebulon's parents, they might stop the pursuit at that point, and it would be safe to get on to the river that night.

Zebulon's father came out of the darkness and into the moonlight with his hands up. "Don't shoot. We turning ourselves in." Zebulon's mother was close behind, clinging to her husband's shirt.

The overseer was drunk. He didn't care whether he brought these two back or not. He lifted his rifle and shot off the foot of Zebulon's father. Zebulon's father fell to the ground, screaming in pain.

Zebulon's mother pleaded with the overseer, but he laughed and shot her too, killing her. Zebulon's father raised himself off the ground and screamed, "Run!" It was a message to the other man and to his son. "Run, Run!" Then he stood up as if he was going to try to run with his one good leg. The overseer took aim, and with one clean shot to the heart, killed Zebulon's father.

Mrs. Whitaker sighed deeply. "This is what I was told by the man who brought Zebulon here."

I sat there stunned. I couldn't imagine what Zebulon felt. Only seven years old. Being told by that man he was going to get them all killed. Then watching his parents die. My eyes filled with tears.

"Sarah, I've watched you with Zebulon. He knows you are his friend. If anyone can reach him, you can."

"But how? Today I tried everything I could think of, and nothing worked."

"You'll find a way."

"I'm not sure I can. I don't know what else to do."

Lionel came in with an armload of kindling and firewood for Mrs. Whitaker's office fireplace. I don't know how long he was standing there. I brushed away my tears. "Miss Sarah? You all right?"

I nodded and left quickly.

I spotted Zebulon by the window, looking out into the dark night sky. I went over to him, knelt down, and hugged him. He didn't pull away. I whispered, "I love you, Zebulon." A tear slid down his face, then he pulled away and ran off.

Oh, Hannah, my heart is breaking for Zebulon.

Your friend,

Sarah

Goose Creek, Virginia

THIRD MONTH 14, 1859

Dear Sarah,

Mother asked me to help Pearl learn to read and at least write her name. She wants to us do all we can to prepare Pearl for her new life. Mother said we should give her a good Quaker name, as a necessary diversion should anyone question her.

I took a slate and chalk up to the third floor to begin our first lesson.

"I'm going to teach you your letters first so you can learn to write your name." I marked in large print the letters A, B, C. Pearl shrank back in fear. You would have thought I had printed the name of the devil himself. Pearl turned toward the wall and continued to shake.

"It's just the alphabet. All words are made up of letters, so you have to start by learning the letters." Pearl flinched. I continued, "I want to teach you enough reading and writing so you can fool the slave catchers."

She still cowered.

"A free colored girl who can read and write is much more likely to make it to Canada to join her father."

Still Pearl kept her back to me. Nothing I would say convinced her.

Finally, I said, "Fine. If you want to get caught by the slave catcher, that's your choice." I slammed the door shut and gave up.

Mother was knitting in the parlor. "She's impossible!" I exclaimed. "She won't help one bit. She won't even give it a try. All I did was write A, B, C on the slate and Pearl got all crazed."

Mother put down her knitting needles and looked at me silently for a moment. Then she simply said, "Well, you will have to find out what is making her so frightened."

"I tried, Mother, I really did."

"Then try again," Mother responded. "And perhaps with a bit of compassion."

I climbed back up the stairs, not at all eager to talk with Pearl again. She sat on the bed, looking at the floor.

When I sat down next to her, she said in a whisper, "Sorry, Miss Hannah."

Remembering Mother's advice about compassion (not my best characteristic), I asked, "What frightened you so when I wrote those letters?"

"When I was young, probably 'bout five or six, I was playing with Master's children. Toby, that's Master's son, he stacked three wooden blocks, each with a letter on it, just like you wrote. One block with A, another with B, and a third one with C. We had a fine time, just stacking those blocks and knocking them down again."

Pearl got very quiet. "And then what?" I asked.

"Then Master rode up on his horse. Watched us. He jumped off his horse and knocked the blocks out of my hands. He grabbed his whip from his saddle. He whipped me over and over till the blood came pouring out my back."

"All because he thought you were trying to learn to read?"

"I s'pose so. Never really understood what happened, but I never played with Toby again."

"Pearl, Master Worthy knew that the key to your freedom was your being able to read, write, and think for yourself. But you're here now. There will be no penalty for learning to write your name or learning to read." I leaned around to look in Pearl's face. "Would you like to learn to write your name?"

Pearl smiled and picked up the chalk. "Would you show me how?"

I showed her how to hold the chalk. Then with my hand over hers, we drew the letter P.

"That's the first letter in your name. P."

Pearl traced it with her finger. "Now this next one is kind of hard to draw." Again, I closed my hand over hers, and as she held the chalk, we drew E. Then together we wrote the letters A and R and L. "That's Pearl! P-E-A-R-L." She traced all the letters one at a time with her finger. "Now you try." I took my hand away.

Pearl scrunched up her face as she concentrated and studied the letters we had written together. Slowly, haltingly, she scratched out her name.

"You did it!"

She flung her arms around me and smiled broadly. "I did it! I wrote my name."

We were both laughing, but then I heard it. The hounds. The patrols were out again, this time in broad daylight.

"Quick. In here." I turned the latch to the tiny door and shoved Pearl inside. Just before I latched it again, I whispered, "Not a sound."

I looked around the room. Only minutes and they would be here. I straightened the bed covers and pushed a chest in front of the little door. I was glad I had emptied the chamber pot that morning. I grabbed the slate and ran downstairs. I put the slate down on the table. Mother was nowhere to be found. She must be at the springhouse or the well. Oh, how I wished Father was here.

I picked up Mother's knitting from her chair and sat down. The men were at the door just steps away, knocking loud and hard on the door.

My heart raced. What should I do? If I ignore them, they'll be suspicious. But what do I say to them? They've never come in the daytime before.

I stood up, and the knitting fell to the floor. I jumped as the knitting needles clanged on the hard pine floors. My hands were clammy, and the doorknob slipped in my hand as I opened the door.

A tall dark-haired man with a scar on his cheek stood with his hat in his hands. "Morning, young lady. My name is Robert Blockett. I work for a Mister Buck Worthy, owner of Oakwood Plantation in South Carolina. Mister Worthy is missing some property that we believe might be hiding out in this area."

I acted confused. "Property?"

"Yes, two slaves. A father named Joseph ran off several months ago with his daughter, Pearl. We tracked them to Culpeper, Virginia,

Ma'am. The sheriff there told us about your place here. Seems like a number of the runaways have stopped by Evergreen before."

Mister Blockett peered inside. I thought he could see right through me. As his eyes scanned the room, I noticed that my slate was facing up with the name Pearl written on it. I thought, Oh no, what if he sees it? My heart raced as he looked around the room. I moved so I would block his view of the table, where my slate was. After surveying the room, Mister Blockett continued, "Doesn't Yardley Taylor live here?"

"Yes. He's my grandfather."

"Well, what I hear is that Mister Taylor has caused quite some consternation in a number of the neighboring counties over the years. The sheriff in Fauquier County told me he has led raids to free slaves in their county. In fact, Sheriff Thompson told me he would be happy to lend me some slave-hunting hounds. But I told him mine are better and have tracked these two for many miles and won't be giving up too soon."

"Sir, what you speak of—these accusations—were made many years ago."

"Are you saying they have no merit?"

"I am saying that these accusations have nothing to do with the so-called property you seek. I imagine they are long gone to freedom by now."

"Oh, perhaps, but then again, they could be just within spitting distance from here," he said as he stared coldly at me. "Good day for now, Ma'am." He tipped his hat, put it back on his head, and mounted his horse. As he rode off, he turned his horse back, stopped, and stared up at the third floor. Could he know?

I closed the door and leaned against it. I could hardly breathe. Moments later, Mother came in through the back door.

"Was that a slave patrol?"

"Worse. It was Blockett, Mister Worthy's personal slave catcher."

Mother's eyes flashed as she stood for several minutes at the door, listening to the sound of Blockett's horse galloping away. Then she spoke calmly. "At nightfall, we need to move Pearl from the house. From what you told me, he'll be back, probably tonight."

Mother stood guard while I ran up to the third floor and let Pearl out of the little room. I told her what happened and that we needed to move her tonight. She looked at me, terrified. "We won't let anything happen to you."

Just as soon as it was dark, Mother and I walked down to the barn. Mother swept away the hay over the trapdoor, and lifted it. I stared into the gaping hole. A small ladder leaned against the side.

Mother beckoned me to go down, and she followed. We freshened the muslin cloth and stuffed it with new hay for Pearl's bed. Mother took a quick inventory of supplies that would be needed.

"Mother, won't it be too cold for Pearl here?"

"No, you would be surprised how a home in the earth even at this time of year can be warm. There are extra blankets for the horses. We'll put some down here as well. There are dried peaches, apples, some salted ham, and a jug of spring water. We will bring Pearl other food each day." She glanced around, making mental notes. "We'll need a clean chamber pot."

When we climbed back out of the tiny room under the floor of the barn, Mother pulled the door back down on the floor and swept hay over it. "Now, Hannah, you must be very careful to do exactly as I do." Mother picked up cow dung and spread it around the door.

"Mother!" I exclaimed. "What in the world are you doing?"

"It throws the dogs off the scent of a human, Hannah. This is very important. Hay alone covering the trapdoor is not enough. And bring in one of the cows. Fresh dung is better. You must not forget."

Sarah, I am frightened. So very frightened.

Your friend,
Hannah

Goose Creek, Virginia

THIRD MONTH 15, 1859

Dear Sarah,

We heard the sounds of the dog patrols coming down the road. Sounded like three, maybe four, hounds. Then I heard horses. I pushed Pearl down the gravel path to the barn as fast as I could.

I swept away the hay, pushed a cow out of the way, and helped Pearl down the ladder into the dark chamber. I urged her to stay still and be very quiet, no matter what happened. I closed the trapdoor and brushed the hay all over it.

I pulled another cow from the water trough outside the barn. The more animals, the better, I thought. It would confuse the dogs. Then I remembered what Mother had told me. I prodded the cow dung with a stick until some of it covered where the door was. Good old Bessie cooperated and delivered a pile of fresh dung right where I needed it. I rushed back to the house and came in the back way.

No sooner was I inside than the sheriff arrived with Mister Blockett. That man gives me the willies, Sarah. His eyes are as black as coal, and that scar on his cheek — well, I don't want to think about how he got that.

Father asked, "What is the meaning of this?"

The sheriff responded, "I know you are a good man, Thomas Brown, but the activities of your father-in-law, Mister Yardley Taylor, are in serious question. There is a rumor that two slaves made their way from Fauquier County to your home here at Evergreen — a father and a daughter. Mister Blockett here has been hired by Mister Worthy of South Carolina to bring back his property. I'm afraid we must search your home, Thomas."

"Do you have the proper warrants?" asked Father. The sheriff showed him the documents. "Go ahead," said Father, standing aside from the door. "You will find nothing out of order here."

My heart was pounding so hard that I just knew they could hear it. They looked quickly through the first floor rooms. Blockett and his men took much longer in the basement. Mother asked me to escort the men upstairs to our bedrooms. "See that they don't take anything," Mother added.

Blockett took his time poking around in each room, opening armoires, sticking his gun under each bed, lifting curtains. He looked at me. "Upstairs?"

"There are two more rooms upstairs, but you will find nothing there."

"Well, we'll see, won't we, little lady?" He took the steps two at a time. I could tell he was frustrated that he had found nothing so far. He seemed convinced that his prey was in the house.

He searched the first room like the rest of them. He even lifted up the rug to see if there was a hiding place in the floor. Then he came into the room where Pearl had been hiding. His eyes narrowed. My heart raced, and I drew in a sharp breath.

"Be my guest."

He glanced around the room. He looked under the bed as he had in the other rooms. He moved the carpet, and looked out the tiny windows to see if someone was hiding on a ledge.

"Open this trunk," he ordered.

I lifted the lid of the steamer trunk that held old clothes. Blockett lifted his rifle and slammed it down into the clothes. I screamed. He did it again. And again.

Within seconds, Father and the sheriff were in the room. "What is the meaning of this?" Father shouted.

I rushed to Father and began to cry. I pointed at Blockett. "That man is evil. He ordered me to open the trunk. I did. Then he stabbed the clothes over and over like he wanted to find someone and kill them."

The sheriff looked at Blockett disapprovingly. "Robert, you have your warrant. No need to scare the Browns here. They're good people. I think you're done here. You've found nothing. It's time to go."

Blockett took one more look around the room. I held my breath. Would he move the chest? If he did, he'd find the little door into the eaves. And the chamber pot! I had forgotten to empty it that morning.

Blockett stared at me. I stared back.

"I told you that there are no slaves here. Now leave," Father said.

The sheriff stepped back, in front of the chest. I breathed a sigh of relief. "Robert, this way," the sheriff said and he pointed to the door.

As Blockett passed by me, he turned and looked at me. I leveled my gaze to stare back at him as coolly as I knew how.

"Check the barn and the creek," he said.

Oh, Sarah, I have never prayed so hard. I prayed for Pearl, that she would not be afraid. I prayed for the Lord to confuse those dogs. And I prayed for my hands to stop shaking. Mother and Father and I stood out on the porch to watch them.

The dogs yelped all the way to the barn as if they were on the trail of a runaway slave, just as they had been trained. Of course, they were on a trail. We had just been there. I leaned in closer to Mother, who held me tightly to her side. We saw them approach the barn—the sheriff with his warrant, and Mister Blockett with his rifle and his dogs. The dogs yelped and strained at their leashes. As soon as they got inside the barn, however, the dogs ran in circles, confused, disoriented. It seemed as if the trail had gone cold at the door of the barn.

The sheriff and Blockett checked the creek in the next field. Soon they were back on our front porch. Mister Blockett narrowed his eyes and said, "Where is Mister Taylor tonight?"

Father replied calmly, "Mister Taylor is in Philadelphia, where he goes every year at this time to purchase seedling trees and plants for the nursery."

Blockett stood for a moment, chewing his tobacco. He spit on the grass and said dryly, "I doubt it."

I was furious. I clenched my fists and stared at Blockett. "Don't you question my father's honesty!"

Blockett burst out laughing. He gave me a pretend salute, and said, "Yes, Ma'am." Then he mounted his horse and rode off. The sheriff apologized to Father, and Father replied that he knew the sheriff was only doing his job.

After the sheriff left, we came inside. Mother warmed a cup of sassafras tea to calm me down. I was no longer frightened. I was angry.

I wanted to go check on Pearl, but Mother said that Blockett might still be watching. Tonight I would have to stay put. She asked if I was ready to go to bed.

"Bed? After that man touched the bed covers? I don't think so."

Father stoked the fire, and said, "Well, then, if you plan to be up all night, I better keep this fire going."

"Mother, I've been thinking. I don't know how much time we have left with Pearl. What do we need to do to get her ready for her journey to Canada?"

"We need to teach her how to avoid capture," Mother responded. "What do you think Blockett and the others will be looking for?"

"A slave girl, about fourteen or fifteen."

"Right. Poor, uneducated, frightened."

"Oh, I see. You think we can fool everyone into believing Pearl is free? Even if she is caught here in a slave state?"

"Sometimes the best disguise is the one no one expects. We must work with Pearl to give her courage," said Mother.

"I've got an idea." I ran upstairs, taking the stairs two at a time. I flung open the trunk that Blockett had just attacked. At the bottom were old composition books from my early days at school.

I ran downstairs and showed them to Mother. "Blockett wouldn't expect Pearl to learn to read and write in such a short time."

Father added, "She'll need a new name too."

"Let's call her Polly. But she needs a last name. One she can remember," said Mother.

I knew immediately. "Williams," I said, "after her brother."

I don't know how much time we have. Grandfather will be back soon. I need to help Pearl learn how to pretend to be a free black in just a short amount of time. Oh, Lord, please help me.

Your friend,
Hannah

Goose Creek, Virginia

THIRD MONTH 16, 1859

Dear Sarah,

Grandfather's back. He says that by now Joseph should be in New York State and crossing over into Canada. Grandfather says the Committee is working on the plan for Pearl, but it may not be ready for another month. Another month, Sarah! That is much too long. What if that Blockett comes back? Surely, the Committee does not expect us to keep Pearl here that long!

Every day when I come home from school, I help Pearl with her writing. She can write her name Pearl now with ease. She struggles a bit with the new name Polly but understands it is for her safety. She was surprised that I chose her last name, but she agreed it was perfect.

I told her that at least her new name has lots of *l*'s in it, so if we are short on time for her to learn to read and write, she can make lots of pretty loops in writing Polly Williams. Mother told me I must teach her cursive, as this would be the way a free, educated black girl in the North would write.

Pearl asked about Tookie. Have you heard anything else?

Your friend,
Hannah

Philadelphia, Pennsylvania

THIRD MONTH 18, 1859

Dear Hannah,

I'm afraid I have bad news. An abolitionist posing as a slave owner tried to purchase Tookie. The man offered $800, but Worthy turned him down flat. That's the going price for a slave girl.

Do not say anything to Pearl yet, as the negotiations will continue. Meanwhile Mother says we should begin the fund to purchase Tookie anyway. She and I have planned a bazaar for Fourth Month, Eighth Day. Mother has solicited many items for the fair by telling her friends the story of Pearl and Tookie. Their story has captured the hearts of our sewing circle. We are still making clothes for the fugitives. The need is great. But we are also sewing silk purses and scarves for sale at the bazaar.

Hannah, ask your grandfather if he's coming to Philadelphia next month. Perhaps he could bring you to visit in time for the bazaar.

I've decided that I cannot reach Zebulon with any plan. It's like the last time at Seven Oaks. I wore myself out trying to suggest things Zebulon could do. Well, maybe reaching Zebulon doesn't have so much to do with what I do for him. I mean, I cannot purchase his freedom, as we will do for Tookie. I need to find a way to set him free from his pain. Maybe that has less to do with doing something and more to do with being with him. I don't know. It's just something I keep thinking about.

Peter Pennington came by the Shelter again today. He and Mrs. Whitaker spent a long time talking. He left without Mrs. Whitaker buying one thing. He picked up his suitcase and hurried out without saying a word to me. I was glad. There's just something about that man that I don't like.

Your friend,

Sarah

Goose Creek, Virginia

Third Month 20, 1859

Dear Sarah,

The lessons continue in earnest. Every day when I get home from school, Pearl and I work on her writing and reading. She is able to write her new name in cursive quite well now.

The most difficult thing for me to help Pearl with is the way she speaks. Frankly, Sarah, she sounds very southern. In fact, she sounds downright South Carolinian. She told me today that she could help me tote the buckets up from the springhouse. I told her she could do no such thing. She could help me carry the buckets, but no toting was allowed.

She calls her old master "marster," and she calls women "missus." She calls her father "Pappy." Actually, I think it is funny when she asks about my grandpappy. I have started to call Grandfather that when I am teasing him. He says he doesn't know who is teaching whom what!

One day, Mother told me we needed to work on Pearl's hair.

"What's wrong with it? It looks fine to me."

"We need to straighten it. The free blacks in the North use hair oil to train their hair to look like white women."

"Why?"

"I'm afraid there is maybe more prejudice in the free states than we'd like to believe. It's their way of being accepted."

Pearl chimed in, "Oh, that's the way it was on the plantation. Sometimes when they was getting ready to sell some of the women slaves, they'd put bacon grease in their hair to slick it back like the white women. Always brought a higher price for the women when they was sold. So are you gonna put bacon grease in my hair? Then, those patrol dogs gonna find me for sure!"

Mother laughed. "Well, we won't straighten your hair until it is time for the disguise, but we have to find something that would work. Perhaps something a bit less smelly than bacon grease."

"I know. Butter. We can thin it with a little vinegar."

Mother thought that would work so we experimented with the concoction until we found just the right mixture so that it wouldn't harden on Pearl's hair or be too greasy.

I am amazed we've been able to keep Pearl's presence here a secret. Now that it is spring, Joshua is around more and more, but Uncle Richard keeps him busy at the foundry during the afternoon when I'm teaching Pearl. Doctor Janney visited Pearl last week. He says she may be ready for the journey in a month. Sarah, I have so much to do. Only one month to teach Pearl the alphabet, to read like a trained school girl, and to speak like a boarding student!

Your friend,
Hannah

Philadelphia, Pennsylvania

THIRD MONTH 21, 1859

Dear Hannah,

Buck Worthy was furious when he learned from Blockett that Joseph made it to Canada. He has doubled the bounty for Pearl—dead or alive. Please be careful, Hannah.

Mister Worthy still refuses to sell Tookie, but at another visit of the imposter slave owner, he told him that, if he were to sell her, he might do so for $1,300. This is the first time he's been willing to set a price. Mother says that that is what we must earn from the bazaar. It is a terribly large amount of money, though.

Today, with Mrs. Whitaker's blessing, I came to the Shelter and told Zebulon he was coming with me. I bundled him up good, put on his mittens, and then held his hand as we walked out the door. He seemed a bit curious, but didn't say anything.

"Ever ride a train, Zebulon?"

His eyes widened, and he shook his head. We walked to the train station. The gleaming marble walls and the steep steps down to the train tracks captured his attention. He took off his mittens to touch the walls and the brass handrails. He seemed surprised by how cold the marble and metal were.

"Two tickets to Cheltenham, please." I handed the station master the money and got two tickets and my change in return.

"Track four, Miss."

We continued down some more stairs until we got to our track. Zebulon looked all around. He closed his eyes to listen to the sounds of the railroad cars pulling into the station.

"All aboard. Points north. Cheltenham. Edge Hill. Shoemakertown."

"That's us, Zebulon." We climbed aboard. "Let's sit here." I selected a bench seat covered in plush red velvet. I pulled back the curtains so Zebulon could see out the window.

The conductor entered our car and called out, "Tickets. Tickets." I gave him our tickets and Zebulon watched as he punched them both and slid them into the metal slot over our heads. "First train ride, son?" Zebulon nodded. "Much faster than a horse."

Zebulon looked at him incredulously. "Really?"

"Really!" he answered. "Well, enjoy your ride."

The train pulled out of the station. Zebulon leaned in close to the window and waited. Soon we were out of the tunnel and into brilliant sunshine. He turned to me and smiled. It's the first smile I've seen in weeks.

We didn't talk the entire way to Cheltenham. Every now and then, I'd reach over and pat his arm or shoulder. I knew he was taking it all in. When we got to the station, he took my hand. We walked up the stairs to the main floor of the station. Samuel and William were there to meet us. Samuel ran to Zebulon and hugged him. Zebulon broke out in a big grin and started talking a mile a minute, telling Samuel everything he had seen.

The entire buggy ride to Seven Oaks, he talked nonstop. Then he had to repeat it all for Graceanna when he got there. Graceanna had lunch ready for us, and I noticed that Zebulon ate everything on his plate. After lunch, he and Samuel dashed outside to play.

That's when I told William and Graceanna what I knew about Zebulon's parents, and how it seems to have affected Zebulon.

"Well, he seems fine today," said Graceanna.

"For today," I said. "I hope it lasts, but his wounds are deep. The cuts on his back are nothing compared to the cuts on his heart."

A few hours later, Zebulon rushed in. "Miss Sarah, will we go home on the train too?" I laughed and told him yes. Zebulon grinned and rushed back out again to find Samuel.

The ride home was just as spellbinding for Zebulon as the ride out to Seven Oaks. When we got back to the Shelter, he threw his arms around me, said "thank you," and then was off to tell the others about his adventure.

I told Mrs. Whitaker he ate a good lunch today. I wondered, though, if this would last. Mrs. Whitaker told me to take things one day at a time. "Rejoice in the victory of today. It will carry you through tomorrow."

Your friend,

Sarah

Goose Creek, Virginia

THIRD MONTH 23, 1859

Dear Sarah,

I can come! Grandfather must see your uncle Robert for more reprints of his Loudoun County map, and he's agreed that I can come with him. I threw my arms around him and said, "Oh, thank you, dear Grandpappy."

Mother will take over Pearl's lessons while I'm gone. All seems quiet here. Word has it that Blockett is still up north somewhere, hoping to get word on Pearl from the other slave catchers and bounty hunters. He assumes she is on the same Liberty Line as her father, just a bit farther behind.

We leave tomorrow for our journey, so I'll just bring this letter, rather than send it in the quilting square. I can't wait to see you!

Your friend,
Hannah

Philadelphia, Pennsylvania

FOURTH MONTH 1, 1859

Dear Father and Mother,

Mother, you will be pleased to see that this letter is carefully hidden in our latest quilting square. Sarah and I made this one together just to show you that I am not neglecting my needlework.

Grandfather met with some of the men today about the plans for reuniting Pearl with her father. He's now safely in Canada at the St. Catharine Settlement.

Sarah and I are amazed at the number of items that have been donated for the bazaar to sell to raise money for Tookie's release. Wouldn't that be a wonderful surprise for Pearl?

Today Sarah took me to the Shelter where she volunteers, and I met Mrs. Whitaker. She asked, "How are your preparations for the bazaar going?"

"Quite well," I said. "Sarah and I are staying up late making purses and cataloging items. I am amazed at how generous people are. We have hundreds of items that have been donated."

"How has Zebulon been?" asked Sarah. "I haven't been able to come down as much this last week, with the bazaar and all."

"He's quiet, withdrawn."

"I was hoping that the way he was the day of the train ride would continue."

"Maybe he will be intrigued with meeting your good friend from Virginia."

"Mrs. Whitaker, this much I know. Zebulon needs a family. I know there is much love here and care for him. He is heartsick, though, and needs to know he belongs to someone."

"Yes, that is true for all the children we are given charge of, but all the more so with Zebulon."

I added, "Sarah told me the horrible way his parents died."

Mrs. Whitaker said, "It may take years of love for that pain to begin to fade away."

Sarah brightened. "I have an idea. It's only two more years before

Zebulon is apprenticed out from here. I mean, when he is nine, won't the Shelter arrange for a place for him to live and to learn a craft?"

"Yes, that is what our charter requires."

"Then why couldn't he begin earlier? If my brother, William, and his family would take Zebulon in, would that be permitted?"

Mrs. Whitaker thought for a moment. "We would have to make an exception, but then, it is a special case. And he does know the family well from your visits."

"And I'd still see him," said Sarah.

"You know, that just might work. I will raise it with the governing board of our orphanage once you have determined if your brother and his wife are in agreement with this plan."

"Mrs. Whitaker, I know this will work! Come on, Hannah, I want you to meet Zebulon."

Sarah was so excited about the plan one minute, and disappointed the next. She tried to get Zebulon to talk to me, but he kept his head down, staring at the floor.

"This is my best friend. She's from Virginia, but she and her family don't believe in slavery. She's helping a little girl about your age escape from a terrible master."

No response.

"Sarah tells me you rode on a train," I said. "Can you tell me about it? What was it like?"

Nothing.

Sarah looked at me. I could see how frustrated she was.

"Well, it's good to meet you, Zebulon," I said. "I hope to see you again sometime."

His eyes didn't budge from the spot he was staring at on the floor.

Sarah knelt down and hugged Zebulon. I could see his shoulders soften some, and he glanced at her for a brief moment. She whispered in his ear something I couldn't hear.

Later I asked her, "What did you say to Zebulon back there, at the end?"

"I just told him what I've been telling him every time I am with him. 'Zebulon, I love you.'"

Tell Pearl I said hello and that Sarah says she can't wait to meet her.

Your daughter,

Hannah

Philadelphia, Pennsylvania

FOURTH MONTH 4, 1859

Dear Father and Mother,

It is very late but I must write you. I am sure you will hear of it soon in the newspapers. Today a Negro from Loudoun County — our county in Virginia — was arrested and brought here to Philadelphia! They say his real name is Daniel Dangerfield. He was arrested under the Fugitive Slave Act and may be returned to his owner in Virginia.

But this man has lived in Pennsylvania for the last nine years. This morning, Mister Dangerfield was at the market, when out of nowhere, a man from Loudoun County identified him, and the marshal arrested him. The marshal yelled out to the crowd that Dangerfield was a thief. If the crowd thought he was arresting Mr. Dangerfield under the Fugitive Slave Act, they would have tried to rescue him right then and there. The marshal handcuffed him and took him to Philadelphia. There will be a trial to determine his fate. Will he remain a free man, or will he be sent back to Virginia to slavery?

A steady stream of people arrived here tonight, talking about what they can do to help.

Your daughter,
Hannah

Philadelphia, Pennsylvania

FOURTH MONTH 5, 1859

Dear Father and Mother,

At First Day services, many spoke out about Mister Dangerfield's predicament. Folks are outraged that a man who has lived here in a free state for nine years could be returned to slavery. Many prayed for justice and righteousness to prevail. The trial begins tomorrow.

There is some talk of trying to raise funds for his purchase if all else fails. They say he would go for around $1,500. Sarah's mother told us that we must be prepared for our bazaar to free Tookie to turn into a fair to raise money for Daniel Dangerfield instead. I want Mister Dangerfield to be free, I truly do. But I also want Pearl's sister to be free. Must one be sacrificed for the other?

I know Sarah's mother is right. How can we have a bazaar in just three days to raise money for purchasing a slave (our Tookie) and ignore the needs of this man who is on trial for his life tomorrow? Yet it hurts. I wish there were a way for both to be free. Sarah and I prayed together tonight for God's mercy and justice to prevail in the trial tomorrow.

Your daughter,
Hannah

P.S. Grandfather and Sarah's father just came in. Grandfather sends you his love. They have decided to attend the trial and take Sarah and me with them! We will get up very early tomorrow, as many people will want to be there to support Mister Dangerfield.

Philadelphia, Pennsylvania

FOURTH MONTH 7, 1859

Dear Father and Mother,

When we arrived, there were hundreds of Negroes at the courthouse at Fifth and Chestnut streets. Marshal Yost swore in fifty special marshals ready for any emergency. Grandfather told me even Marshal Yost disagrees with this arrest. Marshal Yost offered $50 toward the purchase amount and up to $200 if necessary.

The hearing lasted fourteen hours and went on all night! It began at four o'clock yesterday afternoon and was not over until six o'clock this morning. We stayed the entire time.

There were lawyers for both sides and lots of witnesses — one side trying to prove that Daniel Dangerfield is the escaped slave from Virginia, and the other side trying to prove he is not. Some said they knew Daniel as a boy and as a young man in Loudoun, and that this is the same person. A Virginia doctor testified that he had treated a slave owned by the Simpsons for typhoid, and that he recognizes this man, Daniel Dangerfield, as the same man.

There were witnesses for Daniel Dangerfield as well, but to me, they didn't seem as strong. They said they had known Mr. Dangerfield as a free man for years.

Mother, you will never guess who I met yesterday. Sarah introduced me to Friend Lucretia Mott. She was there for the entire trial. She sat right next to Mister Dangerfield. When the attorneys for the slave owner requested that she be removed, she threw her arms around Mister Dangerfield's neck and said she would rather give $100 to rescue him than one cent to purchase him.

A court officer removed Friend Lucretia Mott from beside Mister Dangerfield and asked her to sit in the back of the courtroom. Mother, the attorneys for Mister Dangerfield moved her chair back so it was again next to Mister Dangerfield, and that is where she sat the entire trial. She never left his side.

At a break in the trial, Sarah introduced me to Friend Lucretia. "Sarah has told me much about thee," Friend Lucretia said. "Watch carefully today. There is much you can learn here about the power of righteousness."

I asked, "Do you know Mister Dangerfield?"

Friend Lucretia Mott replied, "I know many Mister Dangerfields. I understand you have met some yourself recently, in the father and daughter sent your way. And now, young Talitha. I look forward to your bazaar."

Grandfather greeted her and said he was glad to see her again. Friend Lucretia said, "It is I who am benefited by being with thee again. I have heard much of thy recent efforts. It is not easy to live in a slave state among slave owners and still speak out for justice. May God continue to bless what thee are doing."

Mother, I cannot describe her. She is so strong of character and of the light of Christ that her whole body reflects it. She sat with Mister Dangerfield as though never tired, no matter how late the trial was going. She sat with her knitting in her lap, her needles clicking away, and all the time staring at Commissioner Longstreth as if she were willing him to make the right decision. She told Grandfather that sometimes old ladies with knitting needles prick the consciences of judges.

She explained that she had arrived early for the hearing and gathered with several women from the anti-slavery society in the basement under the courtroom. There she saw Commissioner Longstreth sitting at a table, writing. Since she knew him to be of Quaker descent, she boldly spoke to him in the earnest hope that his conscience would not allow him to send this poor man into slavery. He was quite civil but replied that he was bound by his oath of office and he must judge fairly.

Nonetheless, I am certain it was her presence in that courtroom that reminded Commissioner Longstreth of a higher duty. It came as no surprise to many when the commissioner issued his order. He said that based on some conflicting testimony, he could not say that this Daniel Dangerfield was the same man who had fled Loudoun County years ago.

The streets were lively with both celebration and outrage. There must have been a thousand Negroes and abolitionists in the streets, rejoicing in the decision to release Mister Dangerfield. But there were an equal number of southern sympathizers, who were furious at his release.

Sarah was surprised to see Nathaniel outside. She called to him, "What are you doing here?"

"And I could ask you the same question," Nathaniel replied. "Probably we'd have the same answer: to see justice done."

Some of the other boys called to him, "Nathaniel, come on. We have to hurry."

He turned to Sarah. "All is not what it seems," he said and then ran off to join the other boys.

We found out later that Nathaniel and these boys came up with the idea to get Mister Dangerfield out of that mob and to safety. Nathaniel and his friends escorted another man, who resembled Mister Dangerfield, to a carriage and drove him off. Meanwhile the real Dangerfield was spirited away in the company of friends.

I told Sarah that I thought Nathaniel is very brave. She agreed.

Your daughter,

Hannah

Philadelphia, Pennsylvania

Fourth Month 8, 1859

Dearest Father and Mother,

It is very late, but I cannot rest until I tell you everything that happened today.

We slept little the last few days, between the trial and readying the goods for the bazaar. Sarah's mother has worked tirelessly. We owe her so much. She received, cataloged, and arranged all the goods for sale. Others from the sewing circle were there to assist, but it was Sarah's mother who gave of her heart and soul all day.

The fair was to begin at ten o'clock. We were at the auditorium by seven to arrange the tables and place cloths over each one. We tagged and displayed the items as Sarah's mother suggested. She has such a flair for display.

The fair opened with great excitement. Everyone there was still full of the joy of the victory in Commissioner Longstreth's court. There was much to celebrate, and the people were in a very generous mood. Often if an item had a price of five dollars, a buyer would give us seven. Or if the asking price for an item was ten dollars, a buyer might give us twenty. It was astonishing to Sarah and me. Many people I was just meeting for the first time wanted to know all about Talitha.

Lucretia Mott stopped by and selected a purse that Sarah had made. Sarah was thrilled and wanted to give it to her. Friend Lucretia clucked her tongue and said, "Dear Friend Sarah, thee would give me this gift from thy heart, but we must both give Talitha a gift by the exchange—you with your beautiful stitchery and me with my coins. Together we will help set her free."

Sarah said she felt as if she were dancing on air. Of course, I know that we Quakers do not dance, but sometimes we feel like it.

Then Friend Lucretia took me by the hand and led me to a small stage. I was unprepared for what happened next. Friend Lucretia,

the little woman with the big voice, got the attention of the crowd. All the bazaar activity stopped, and a hush fell over the room.

Friend Lucretia pushed me gently in front of her and said, "Hannah Brown has a few words to say about young Talitha, for whom we will buy many items today at this bazaar. Hannah?"

I looked out over the crowd. Everyone was staring at me, waiting for me to speak. My mouth was dry, my hands were damp, and my heart raced. Friend Lucretia whispered in my ear, "Just tell them her story."

And so I began. "Talitha is very young, maybe only six. It's hard to know. It seems that slaves know more about what price they would fetch than how old they are.

"She is all alone. Her mother died, and her father has disappeared. Her brother and sister are gone too. There is no one to look out for her and to take care of her. She takes care of the master's baby. She's just a baby herself.

"If we do not help her, she will only know a life of slavery. We can purchase her freedom. She can grow up to know what we all know. She won't have to look over her shoulder and wonder, Is this the day I am whipped or beaten or sold away? Thank you all so much for what you are doing here today to raise money to purchase Talitha."

As the audience applauded, Friend Lucretia came forward again and placed her hand on my shoulder. She leaned in, and said, "When they hear the stories, their hearts are moved, and they buy more purses." I looked at her in surprise, but she was right. We collected $1,327, more than enough to purchase Tookie!

Grandfather and Sarah's father arrived to help us put away the tables. Then they took us to a large anti-slavery meeting at Samson Hall to celebrate Daniel Dangerfield's release. Mr. Purvis was there. So was Friend Lucretia. Many members of the Committee were there. Grandfather pointed out to me these notable men and women. I felt as if I were in the presence of angels.

Father, there were also some very rude southerners present.

They created such a disturbance by stamping, hallooing, groaning, and hollering that it was impossible to hear the speakers. At one point the hecklers rushed forward toward the speakers at the podium. Grandfather held Sarah and me close to him. I don't know whether I was excited or fearful; my emotions have been in such a whirlwind for the last few days. At last the police arrived and arrested some of the disturbers.

We did not come back to the Smiths' house until very late. I could not rest, though, until I had written to you.

With love,

Hannah

Goose Creek, Virginia

FOURTH MONTH 17, 1859

Dear Sarah,

Joshua came by when I got back to Evergreen. I didn't tell him everything, as I am still not sure where he stands on the issue of slavery. He asked about the Dangerfield trial, as he had heard from Uncle Richard that we were there.

The local papers here, both the *Washingtonian* and the *Democratic Mirror,* printed much of the testimony of the witnesses, so Joshua knew quite a bit about it. The newspapers even spoke about Lucretia Mott, but they did not tell the whole story.

You should have seen Joshua's face when I described Friend Lucretia with her knitting needles clicking and clacking as a constant reminder to Commissioner Longstreth that he should do the right thing.

I was surprised how much I missed spending time with Pearl. Mother brought her back to the third floor while we were gone. I told Pearl the whole story about Daniel Dangerfield.

I love Pearl's stories. She is quite funny now that she is willing to talk.

"Miss Hannah, master's overseer loves to blow the horn. He'd blow it for us to wake up, blow the horn for us to come to the field, blow the horn for a meal break, and blow the horn to stop working. Just like this."

Pearl puffed up her cheeks and her eyes bugged out while she made trumpeting noises in her throat. I kept telling her to hush, but I was laughing so hard. I am surprised no one found us.

"Did they make you work on Christmas?" I asked.

"Well, if you were a house slave, there was much to do. But they start celebrating the week before Christmas and don't stop until New Year's Day. The master had folks over for all sorts of banquets and dances." Her eyes danced. "Last year, they told me to

help the house servants at the big house. When I first came into the kitchen, I saw pies lining the pantry shelves. Mince pies. Apple pies. Cakes. Nothing like the little bag of sweets they give us slaves on Christmas Day."

"What did you do?"

"I just smelled all those smells. I couldn't move. I stood there and watched the house servants carry in legs of mutton and venison and long links of sausages. Bowls of eggnog were filled high with thick cream and sprinkled with spices. The slave in charge of the kitchen told me I better get on my apron and help out before she sent me out to the fields. Only then did I stop staring and get to work."

"We Quakers treat Christmas like any other First Day."

"You mean simple, right?" Pearl asked. "Well, it shore wasn't simple at the big house. They put a tall green cedar tree that reached to the ceiling in the entrance hall. They decorated it with ropes of colored paper chains, and garlands of popcorn and berries. The tree had lighted candles made on the plantation from the wax of marsh myrtle berries." Pearl's eyes sparkled as she told me about it.

"So," I asked, "what about the slaves? What was their Christmas like?"

"Oh, Miss Hannah, heaps different. Slaves don't have to work on Christmas Day, so they can have their parties too. After the praise gatherings where we worship together, we usually had a picnic by the river."

"What kinds of food would you eat?"

"Nothing like master did. But we had a good spread anyway. An Edisto River slave knows the rivers, creeks, marshes, and backwaters, and no one ties as strong a fishing net as a slave. We'd eat crabs, clams, and oysters for our Christmas dinner, along with a captured rabbit or possum."

"Sounds good to me!"

"It was, but that day, Miss Hannah, when I was helping in the master's kitchen, oh how I wanted to taste that mutton, drink a cup of eggnog, and eat some spicy mince pie."

"Mince pie is awful," I said.

"Oh, don't tell me that. It looked so good."

The doctor has pronounced Pearl fit to travel, and I told her it would soon be time for her to continue on her journey and join her father. I will miss her. I realized though that Pearl's talking was not so southern anymore. Maybe, just maybe, she can pass for a northern girl.

Doctor Janney told me he heard that Mister Blockett is back in town. The name of that man sends shivers down my spine. If I never see him again, that will be too soon.

> *Your friend,*
> *Hannah*

Philadelphia, Pennsylvania

FOURTH MONTH 19, 1859

Dear Hannah,

We drove out to Seven Oaks last First Day to be with Graceanna, William, and of course, Samuel and Jonathan. It was good to have the whole family together. Most of my visits to Seven Oaks over the last number of months have been from the Shelter with Zebulon.

When they asked about him, I made sure Samuel was outside and Jonathan was down for his nap. Then I told them his story. Mother and Graceanna wept.

Father sighed and said, "That's why we do what we do, but change does not come fast enough."

William, however, before I could even ask, said, "Graceanna, we have to do something. Zebulon should live with us. That boy needs the love of a family. He and Samuel are fast friends. There's always room for one more here."

I looked hopefully at Graceanna. She seemed troubled. "Well, I was going to tell you this later today, but William, there will be one more here. I am with child."

Mother clapped her hands, and said, "Blessings on you, dear one." William whisked her up in his arms and kissed her, right there in front of us.

Father added, "Congratulations, you two."

I wondered, though, why Graceanna seemed troubled. Wasn't that good news?

"Sarah, I love Zebulon. I do," said Graceanna. "But right now might not be the best time to bring Zebulon into our home. With a new baby and all. Jonathan is such a handful."

"I'm sure Zebulon wouldn't be any trouble at all," I said. "And he and Samuel could spend lots of time together. I'd be here to help too."

"Yes, but Sarah, Zebulon needs special attention, extra attention, and I'm just not sure I can give it right now. Perhaps in a year."

William stood by his wife and put his hand on her shoulder. "Sarah, we'll talk more about this, but it may be a question of timing, not a question of willingness."

I pleaded, "But there may not be time to wait. Zebulon turns more and more inside himself. He needs the special love of a family now, more than ever."

Father stood and said, "This is a matter for William and Graceanna to discern. Let them discuss it—in private. It's time for us to return to Philadelphia anyway."

I was quiet all the way home. I thought it had been such a wonderful idea—Zebulon going to live with William and his family. I am happy for William and Graceanna, really I am, but disappointed too.

Father left me alone with my thoughts until we pulled the buggy up in front of our home. As I opened the door to get out, he said, "God loves Zebulon more than you do. You must trust he has a plan, even when you cannot see it."

I nodded, but truth be told, I didn't really believe it.

Your friend,

Sarah

Philadelphia, Pennsylvania

FOURTH MONTH 21, 1859

Dear Hannah,

I talked with Charlotte Forten tonight at an anti-slavery society meeting. She told me Daniel Dangerfield is now safe, living in Canada. I knew you'd want to know.

We got word tonight that Mister Worthy might be willing to sell Tookie, but the price is now $1,800. Much more than we earned from the fair.

Father said that there are those who are concerned about paying such a high price. It makes it harder for them the next time they are trying to purchase family members for those who have already escaped.

Nathaniel came by today, and I told him about our plan for Tookie. I didn't realize we had so much in common, until I saw him that night after the Dangerfield trial. He's been working with a group of high school boys who help out the Committee whenever they are asked. They drive buggies, deliver messages, build secret rooms in safe houses, and act as decoys.

He told me he heard I wanted to be a doctor. I was shocked.

"Who told you that?"

"Dad. I mean, Principal Ivins. He said that we're going to have physiology lectures next year—at the Boys' School. He told me that there was going to be one girl at least who would be disappointed. I figured it was you."

"You did? How?"

"Sarah, you're the only one I know who has taken every science class the school has offered. When we have guest lectures in science, you are there. You carry around borrowed science textbooks with you." Then he smiled. "Besides, your father talked to my father about it."

I laughed. "Oh, so you're not that perceptive, after all."

"Well, no."

"What did your father think?"

"I overheard him telling your father that you have a keen mind, an earnest spirit, and he recommended that he support you in your quest."

"He did?"

"Absolutely."

"And what do you think?"

"I think you should follow your heart. If you want to be a doctor, then don't let anything stand in your way. I'll loan you my physiology book next year, if you like."

Can you believe it? Nathaniel does not think it is strange that I want to be a doctor! And who knows? Maybe his father can convince mine to let me go to medical college.

Your friend,

Sarah

Philadelphia, Pennsylvania

FOURTH MONTH 24, 1859

Dear Hannah,

I went to the Shelter today. Peter Pennington was there again. He had his suitcase full of wares with him. Mrs. Whitaker talked to him for a long time and selected only a comb for purchase.

When it looked as though she was completing her purchase, I stepped into her office to ask her if I could take Zebulon to the park. Mr. Pennington rose and said, "Good day, Miss Sarah."

"Good day."

"It's a beautiful day. So you're going to take Zebulon outside?"

My eyes narrowed. Why should he care?

Mr. Pennington turned toward Mrs. Whitaker. "I'd be happy to accompany them to the park, if you like."

Mrs. Whitaker responded, "That's all right. I'm comfortable with Sarah taking Zebulon out for a walk."

I was glad she said that. Mr. Pennington gives me the creeps.

Zebulon was quiet on our walk to the park. I brought a ball that we kicked around for a while. He seemed dispirited though. I wish Samuel had been with us.

Later I suggested we sit down under a tree while I cut up some apple slices for him. As he munched on them, I said, "Zebulon, Mrs. Whitaker told me what happened to your parents." He stopped chewing for a moment, and said nothing. "I just wanted you to know."

We sat in silence together for another half hour. I put my arm around him and pulled him in closer. He didn't pull away.

Before I stood up when it was time to go, I once again whispered to him, "I love you, Zebulon."

William and Graceanna are still thinking about whether Zebulon can move in with them. Mrs. Whitaker says that even if they are willing to have him with them, the orphanage may not be able to release him until he is nine years old.

I don't know what God's plan is, but I wish he would hurry up.

Your friend,

Sarah

Goose Creek, Virginia

FOURTH MONTH 30, 1859

Dear Sarah,

Tonight Grandfather told us he will take Pearl with him to Philadelphia, disguised in Quaker dress. The large bonnet will hide her face, and if he takes the back roads, he will likely avoid discovery. Once in Philadelphia, Pearl will be turned over to others to continue her journey up the Liberty Line. I hope you will meet Pearl when she comes to your city.

I begged Grandfather to let me go too, but he says it is much too dangerous. There are now nightly dog patrols. News of Daniel Dangerfield's successful trial has spread. Other slave owners here in Loudoun County think that will encourage other slaves to run away from here too. The slave owners are meeting to discuss what they can do to stop the flood of runaways from crossing the river. Grandfather says the borders will be especially well guarded. He leaves tomorrow night with Pearl.

I helped Father ready the wagon for their journey. I guess I shouldn't have been surprised when I saw a false floor in the bed of the wagon. If necessary, Grandfather can hide Pearl under the wagon flooring. What a horrible place to ride! A wagon ride while sitting on the buckboard on these back roads shakes one to the bones as it is. I tried to make the false space as comfortable for Pearl as possible, just in case. I spread out Frank's old blanket and put some hay in a muslin cloth bag for a little pillow. Father and I readied the supplies: food, water, and of course Grandfather's maps.

I gave Pearl her last reading lesson. She is getting better, but I do not think she could hold her own if challenged. I showed her how to tie her bonnet and secure her kerchief around her shoulders. We hugged good-bye. Pearl said she would never forget the kindness of my family. I said I would never forget Pearl and that she was not to worry about Tookie. We would not stop trying to purchase her from Mister Worthy.

I will give Joshua this letter to post for me, as he is going to town for Uncle Richard. We have much to do tonight. Note the horrible stitches in this quilt square. Alas!

Your friend,
Hannah

On the Way to Philadelphia

FIFTH MONTH 2, 1859

Dear Sarah,

When darkness came over Evergreen, Mother and I went down to the barn with Pearl. Mother adjusted the big bow on Pearl's bonnet. Pearl threw her arms around Mother and didn't want to let go. Pearl and I hugged good-bye again, and Father helped her get up into the wagon to sit next to Grandfather on the buckboard. I handed him his ear trumpet, which he settled on the floorboard next to his feet. "Take good care of your package, Grandpappy," I whispered as he flicked the reins. The horses began to pull the wagon up the hill.

Father, Mother, and I returned to the house. Mother and I did some sewing, but my heart was not in it. Mother asked me to go to the springhouse to bring up some milk. After I pulled up the jug of milk from the cool waters, I heard them. Dogs. Barking loudly. Coming down from North Fork. Patrols, Sarah. With Grandfather only two hours away! I knew he could not have traveled that far.

Suddenly I remembered I had not secured the trapdoor in the barn. I ran to the barn to close it. The cattle were not anywhere near the barn, and I had to get one into the barn to help disguise the scent. I chased old Bessie down from the hill and tugged on her lead to get her in there.

From down the hill, I saw the outline of a man with dogs at the door of our home. Father was speaking with him. Blockett!

The dogs were going crazy now because of the fresh scent of Pearl. Blockett must have realized he was onto something and gave the dogs a longer lead. They tore at their leashes and raced to the barn. I was terrified and hid around the corner. The dogs bared their teeth and snarled and strained at their leashes.

Blockett raised his kerosene lantern high and spied the fresh wagon wheel ruts in the ground. The sheriff, holding the reins of Blockett's horse, a fine chestnut stallion, caught up with Blockett at our barn; he too saw the wagon wheel ruts. Blockett handed the dogs' lead lines to the sheriff, and I overheard him tell him he'd be back for them later. He mounted his horse, kicked his sides, and galloped off, following the wagon tracks.

When the sheriff left with the dogs, I ran back into the house. I was crying and carrying on something awful. I was so frightened for Grandfather and Pearl. That stallion would have no trouble catching up with Grandfather. His old plow horses pulling the weight of the wagon, even with a two-hour lead, would be no match for that muscled beast. I hated him, Sarah. I hated Blockett with everything in me. Father tried to calm me down but I wouldn't be calmed. "Father, we have to do something to warn Grandfather."

There was a swift knock at the door. It was Joshua. His horse was tied to our fencepost. "Friend Thomas Brown, I know all about it. I have known for months." I must have looked shocked, for he said to me, "Your grandfather placed his faith in me." Then he turned to Father and said, "Now I ask you, sir, to place your faith in me as well."

"What are you suggesting?" Father asked.

"I was returning from town when I saw Friend Yardley. I shouted a hello to him. He tipped his hat in my direction, but the Quaker girl riding beside him did not so much as wave at me. When I saw Hannah, I knew that the young lady with Friend Yardley was not your daughter."

"No," Father said carefully. "It wasn't."

Then Joshua turned to me and said, "Hannah, you do not like your bonnet. I knew that if you were with your grandfather, you would not have your head covered as that girl did. Then when I heard the dog patrols, I came here immediately. The man who flew away from here on the mighty stallion—I assume he is after Friend Yardley and his charge?"

"Yes," said Father. "He is a slave catcher from South Carolina."

"Then you must trust me. I have a plan, but there is no time to waste. I am fond of Friend Yardley and do not want to see him arrested. But there is only one aspect of my plan to which you must agree—Hannah must ride with me."

"Me ride with you!"

Joshua explained to Father. "The wagon will slow Friend Yardley down significantly. The slave catcher on that fine horse should be able to catch him, but if I can get there first, then Hannah can change places with the slave."

Father asked, "However will you do that?"

"Friend Yardley has not only taught me to survey the roads, but he has taught me the back roads. Those many days of journeying with him have paid off. He showed me a shortcut to the river. It is not one that the slave catcher will know, as he will be following the wagon tracks and keeping to ordinary roads." Joshua glanced over his shoulder. "Even if the man knows a quick way to the river, he does not know what I know. Friend Yardley taught me about paths many do not know, which he has used for his activities through the years. He'll have to stick to the regular roads with his wagon, but I can catch up with him by the shortcuts."

Father looked at Mother, and she nodded.

"We must hurry," Joshua said. "There is no time to waste." He untied his horse and swiftly mounted him.

Father gave me a leg up onto Joshua's horse, and Mother grabbed one of my bonnets and handed it to me. "You may need this" was all that she said. There was no time for good-byes as Joshua kicked Lightning into a gallop. Lightning was true to his name, and I clung tightly to Joshua as we rode swiftly through the night.

Joshua leaned low in the saddle, urging Lightning to go faster and faster. We rode through unkempt paths where I ducked my head behind Joshua to try to avoid the branches as they whipped by. We rode through creeks. We rode and rode and rode—hard and fast.

Joshua pulled up on Lightning.

"What's wrong?"

"I don't know. I thought the shortcut was here. It looks so much different in the pitch dark of night."

Joshua trotted slowly along the road, searching for the entrance to the path. I swallowed hard and tightened my grip around Joshua's waist. "God, please help us," I whispered.

Joshua doubled back. Suddenly he saw it and kicked Lightning's sides. In a moment, we were down the hill and through a creek. Joshua urged Lightning on and kept checking the stars. He pulled up on Lightning again and said, "There, see that clearing?" And moments later, we were back on the main road.

A few miles before the river, we caught up with Grandfather's wagon. Joshua helped me down and up into the wagon.

"Blockett's not far behind. We have to hurry," I explained. "Pearl, switch places with me. Hurry!" I held the reins of the horses while Grandfather helped Pearl up onto Lightning, behind Joshua.

"Meet us at the path near the creek up from Edward's Ferry," said Grandfather.

Joshua nodded and raced down the darkened path with Pearl clinging to him.

Grandfather flicked the reins, and we continued at a fast clip down the road. I barely had time to tie my bonnet in place before Blockett reined in his stallion, soapy with sweat from a fast gallop, right next to our wagon. My heart, which had started beating fast in the springhouse, was racing now. I kept my head down. Grandfather had told me that he would do all the talking, and for that I was grateful.

Blockett raised his pistol and shouted at Grandfather, "Halt!" Grandfather whoaed the horses to a stop and turned to Blockett. "Where are you going?" barked Blockett. "And who is that there with you?"

Grandfather said, "What authority have you to brandish your weapon like that?"

Blockett replied, "I have a warrant from the sheriff's office for the capture and arrest of two slaves, one of whom you have there with you."

Grandfather said, "Man, you will scare my granddaughter with all these theatrics. Put down your gun. How dare you! Who are

you to threaten me with lies and accusations? Don't you have more important business to attend to?"

"You are my business," replied Blockett. His voice made my skin grow cold. "You and that supposed granddaughter there. You, girl—show your face."

Grandfather spoke gently to me. I was shaking. "Do not answer this man's commands. He is not thy father nor thy grandfather."

I leaned in closer to Grandfather. He seemed so calm and confident. I wondered why he didn't want me to look at Blockett. After all, once he saw it was me and not Pearl, wouldn't that settle things? Then I realized what Grandfather was doing. He was trying to stall to give Joshua time to get away.

I was scared, but I knew what Grandfather wanted me to do. I was sure Blockett could hear my heart beating.

Turning to the slave catcher, Grandfather said sternly, "You show your face first."

Blockett lifted his lantern, and the light glowed on his wizened face. I shuddered as I stole a glance at him from under the brim of my bonnet.

Grandfather said, "Ah, Mister Blockett, I presume. I have heard a lot about you but have not had the pleasure of meeting you. I understand you have visited with my family, though. Mister Blockett, the persons whom you seek are not with me." Grandfather shook his head slowly. "Why don't you trouble some other poor soul, and leave me and my granddaughter alone? We have many miles to keep until we arrive at our friend's home by her bedtime."

"That is not your granddaughter!" Blockett bellowed. At that he kicked his horse, rode near my side of the wagon, and snatched at my bonnet, which was tied securely under my chin. I lurched away from Blockett and leaned closer to Grandfather.

"If you dare lay a hand on my granddaughter again, I will wallop you good, gun or no gun. We Quakers are a peace-loving people, but I will not stand for any harm to come to my granddaughter." Grandfather then turned to me and said, "Please

remove thy bonnet and speak to this poor excuse for a man. Tell him thy name."

With trembling hands I untied my bonnet. My hair, which had been pinned up before my ride on Lightning, fell around my shoulders. Blockett's lantern shone in my eyes as I said firmly, "I am Hannah Maria Brown, daughter of Thomas and Elizabeth Brown, and granddaughter of Yardley Taylor."

Blockett was stunned. He turned his horse and headed off.

Fifteen minutes later, I was thrilled to see Joshua and Pearl standing by Lightning at our appointed meeting place. Grandfather planned to take his wagon across the Potomac River by ferry, because a certain ferryman was on duty. The man was a friend to the Friends on the Underground Railroad.

Joshua and Grandfather spoke quietly while I told Pearl what had happened. Then Grandfather told me that I must come with him to Philadelphia. It would not do for Blockett to return to Evergreen tomorrow to find me there. Also, Joshua said it was too dangerous for Pearl to ride up front on the buckboard, with Blockett on their trail. I could help Grandfather hide Pearl away when necessary.

Joshua touched my arm. "I will tell your mother and father that you are safe and all is well," he said.

I looked at Grandfather and asked, "Won't Mother and Father disapprove? After all, they think I am only going to the river with Joshua."

"I almost forgot," said Joshua and pulled a bundle from his saddle bag. "Your mother gave me this and said, 'It's for Hannah—for her trip.'"

I untied the string around the cloth bundle. There was a slate, chalk, and the composition book.

"We can continue our lessons!" said Pearl.

I smiled as I realized that Mother knew all along what might happen. Grandfather shook Joshua's hand. "You will make a fine surveyor one day. You know the hills and hideaways as well as I do."

Joshua mounted Lightning and said to me, "I will expect some apple pie when next I see you." I felt myself blush. He winked at Grandfather, turned Lightning, and raced back toward Goose Creek.

Grandfather, Pearl, and I arranged ourselves in the wagon and headed for the ferry just another mile away. We all got a good laugh when we told Pearl about Blockett's face when I took off my bonnet. "He was expecting a black face for sure and certain!" declared Pearl.

When we neared the ferry, Grandfather went ahead by himself. He came back and said, "All is arranged." He helped Pearl into the secret compartment in the wagon, and we were able to cross the Potomac River into Maryland without further incident. Grandfather hurried the horses on until we reached Pennsylvania. He pulled over to let Pearl out.

"Breathe deep, young lady. Breathe the fresh air of freedom." Pearl was so excited that she gave out a whoop, jumped down from the wagon, and kissed the ground.

Soon we will be in Philadelphia. Oh, Sarah, then I will deliver this letter to you in person. Yet I think that when Grandfather tells the story, it will become somewhat embellished and all the better for the telling. I can't wait to see you. And now you will meet Pearl.

Your friend,
Hannah

Philadelphia, Pennsylvania

FIFTH MONTH 15, 1859

Dearest Father and Mother,

The first night we arrived, Sarah's father hid Pearl in the attic eaves in a specially built secret room. He moved a chest in front of the small door after Sarah and I gave Pearl a blanket and some food. Sarah's father said that lately slave catchers with warrants have been able to search the homes of several families known to assist fugitives. Fortunately, no one has been captured, but he did not want to take any chances with Pearl.

Grandfather said that Mister Blockett won't take long to figure out we're not in Virginia anymore. Grandfather fears some folks in Loudoun County who aren't too happy with his abolitionist activities might suggest to Blockett they can find him in Philadelphia working with abolitionist sympathizers. Once he gets here, he will make inquiries and learn of our friendship with the Smiths.

Sarah's father left to arrange the next stop for Pearl on her journey north to Canada. Sarah and I were so glad that we had the day with Pearl. We took a basket of food upstairs for her. I worked with Pearl on her reading.

At one point there was a loud, urgent knock on the front door. Sarah and I looked at one another in fright. We pushed Pearl back into the small room under the eaves and put the basket of food in with her. We shut the little door and pushed the chest in front of the door.

Sarah went to the doorway and listened at the top of the steps. We were all much relieved when Sarah said it was a Friend. We opened the door and told Pearl to stay there while we went to see what message he might bring regarding her passage to Canada. We moved the chest back in front of the door, just in case anyone else should arrive.

When we reached the bottom of the stairs, we heard this Friend say, "Your young charge is not safe here. The committee received word that the slave catcher, Blockett, has arrived in Philadelphia and is making inquiries. He has money to buy information. Pearl must not stay another night."

"Friends James and Lucretia Mott said it would be their pleasure to receive Pearl into their home at Roadside and forward her on the line. Friend Lucretia remembers fondly the efforts of Sarah and Hannah in the cause of freedom. I will return this evening after dark for Pearl."

I went upstairs and pushed the chest aside, opened the door, and told Pearl the news that she would stay with the Motts that night and then leave to join her father in Canada. Pearl said, "You aren't going with me?"

"No, I wish I could."

Sarah added, "You can trust these Friends with your life. I know them well."

"They will send you from home to home among those who believe, as does Grandfather, in your God-given right to freedom. These Friends are called abolitionists." Pearl's eyes filled with fear. "What's wrong, Pearl?" I asked.

"In the South we were told that abolitionists are people who will kidnap us and sell us."

"Who told you that?"

"Why, Master said it was true."

"Pearl, what Master Worthy said is anything but the truth. *Abolitionist* is a word that comes from *abolish*—it means 'get rid of.' These people want to get rid of slavery forever, and that is why they risk their own safety to make sure you reach freedom. Do not fear; these abolitionists are your friends. Master Worthy didn't want you to know that."

I told Pearl that I had a note in my pocket that Sarah's father had given me the night before. It was a note written by an abolitionist. I read it to her:

Dear Pearl,

I am safe and in the Promised Land. This is Freedom Land, Pearl. The land of Canaan we sang about together with your mammy. There are friends who will bring you to me. I will see you soon. Then together, somehow, we will free your sister. Remember this: "Be strong and of good courage; be not afraid, neither be thou dismayed: for the Lord thy God is with thee wheresoever thou goest."

Pappy

"Pappy made it to Canada?" Pearl said, her eyes brimming with tears.

I nodded. "He had the abolitionist write down what he said so you could keep it in your pocket. I know you cannot read it, Pearl, but I will read it to you over and over until you leave tonight, so you can memorize it. It will comfort you when you are afraid."

I gave Pearl one more reading lesson and wished I had time for more. I do not know why I sense such urgency in this matter. Yet, like you, Mother, I am trying to learn to pay attention to these urges of the Spirit.

That night, after dark, a Friend came to take Pearl to the Motts' farm at Roadside. Grandfather explained to us that Pearl would be sent from farm to farm along the Liberty Line, from Philadelphia to Bristol to Bensalem to Quakertown to Doylestown to Buckingham to New Hope and across the Delaware River to Lambertville, New Jersey. After that, the most dangerous part of her journey would begin.

They would move her from Trenton to Jersey City to Newark to New York. There were many spies in that area of New Jersey, as well as some proslavery sympathizers. The slave hunters' headquarters is right there in New Brunswick about thirty miles before New York.

I asked Sarah's father why they would send Pearl by that route if it is so dangerous. He told us that it is still the fastest route to New York

City, and then the train will take her directly to Rochester and on to Canada. With Blockett hot on the trail and a bounty on her head, the faster they move this package to its final destination, the better.

The next morning, Sarah and I insisted on seeing Pearl again before she left. Sarah's father took us in the buggy to Roadside. He greeted Friend Lucretia, and then excused himself to visit William and his family at Seven Oaks. Friend Lucretia invited us into her parlor. She poured us each a cup of tea.

"Sugar, Pearl?"

"Why, I do think I shall."

We burst out laughing.

"Hannah, I think thy lessons are just about finished." Turning to Pearl, Friend Lucretia added, "Thee will be fine."

Sarah gave Friend Lucretia the latest news on Tookie. "It seems that every time we think we have enough money, Mister Worthy raises the price."

"Perchance, it may take another way."

"What do you mean?" asked Pearl.

"When these negotiations develop into a battle of bids, sometimes it is best to try another approach."

"Such as?" asked Sarah.

"Sometimes, we must be as sly as the slave owner."

When it was time to say good-bye, Sarah and I gave Pearl our presents. Sarah had made her an impressive disguise. We made her try it on. With her hair tucked under the cap, she looked like a Quaker boy. I taught her to hook her thumbs in her new britches and swagger as I had seen Joshua do. We all laughed.

I gave Pearl a bundle that held her slate and chalk and composition book. It was hard to say good-bye. Pearl has become like a dear sister. Friend Lucretia led us in a time of prayer for Pearl and her journey.

When Sarah and I got back to her home, Grandfather said he had hoped to meet with Sarah's uncle about his next map project.

"Alas, Robert just left for a project in New York City that

will last several months. He is working on a map of New York." Grandfather looked out the window, and added, "Oh, how I would love to travel to New York City to see what he is doing. Mapping a city that large, that complex, would be a delightful challenge." He thought another moment, then brightened. "Yes, I think I shall go to New York. Besides, that way I can make sure Pearl makes it safely to the city. Now we must discuss how to get thee back to Virginia."

"Grandfather, take me with you!"

"Heavens, child! Thy parents would have my hide."

"Grandfather, they would be fine with it as long as I am with you."

"Yes, but I might have to help Sarah's uncle with his work." I could tell Grandfather hoped that would be the case. He'd love a chance to work on a map like that.

"True. But who is your best helper? I'm an excellent note taker and can assist you both."

"Child, thee wears me down. Yes, thee may go."

Your adventurous daughter,

Hannah

Philadelphia, Pennsylvania

FIFTH MONTH 17, 1859

Dear Hannah,

No sooner had you left on the train to New York than we received distressing news from the committee about Tookie. Mister Worthy has changed his mind again. He now wants $3,000 for Tookie. Mother is helping me with another bazaar, but I am discouraged.

The Committee says that a direct sale is not likely. It cannot pay such outrageous prices. Their suggestion is to wait for six months or a year until Mister Worthy realizes Joseph is not going to come back for his daughter, and then try to buy her again.

I don't know what Joseph would think of this plan. My guess is that he will risk his own life to come back to South Carolina to rescue her, rather than wait for a year to try to buy her.

It is beautiful here now with all the flowers in bloom. Lionel was willing to drive Zebulon and me out to Seven Oaks. William met the wagon when we arrived, and told Zebulon and Lionel they had much work to do today to ready some of the fields for planting.

"Zebulon," said William, "do you think you are ready to do some man's work today?"

Zebulon's eyes widened. He stood up straight and tall, and said, "Yes, sir. I'm a-ready!" Then he added, "Samuel too?"

"Samuel too. But I'm counting on you. You're older, and stronger too."

Zebulon jumped down from the wagon and, looking back at Lionel, said, "Come on. We got work to do!"

I laughed, and it filled my heart with joy to see Zebulon come alive. It just has to work out for Zebulon to live here with William and Graceanna. It would be perfect.

While the men (and the sure-do-want-to-be men) walked off into the fields, I visited with Graceanna. I desperately wanted to ask her what she was thinking about Zebulon, but remembered

Father's caution to let William and Graceanna decide without any interference.

"How are you feeling these days?"

"I need to nap a lot, but I am feeling well. Thank you. Jonathan takes all my energy."

He was tugging at Graceanna's skirt and pulling her toward the window. He definitely wanted to be with the men.

"Friend Lucretia wanted you to visit today. I'd love to go with you, but ... well ..."

"Jonathan!" I finished.

Graceanna sent me off down the road with a basket of fresh flowers for Roadside. When I arrived, Friend Lucretia was out in her garden. I joined her, and the two of us weeded for several hours.

"I can't wait for the berries. Blackberries. You do know I make the best blackberry pie around, don't you?" She snipped away the weeds from a few more vines, then turned to me and asked, "So, tell me about thy doctoring. What are you learning from Dr. Dixon?"

"Not too much. Other than stitching up Zebulon, we've had mostly sniffles and tummy aches. One day, though, Andrew MacPherson was horsing around outside while climbing a tree. He fell and broke his arm."

"Oh, dear!"

"Mrs. Whitaker sent Lionel to fetch the doctor. He was in surgery and couldn't come until that night. Andrew was in terrible pain and could not stop crying. I asked Mrs. Whitaker if I could wrap his arm."

"That was brave of you."

"Oh, I was nervous! Andrew was screaming in agony. If I could just take the pressure off, I thought, maybe the pain would lessen until Dr. Dixon could get there to help. I studied Andrew's arm and thought about what I could use for a makeshift splint. Wood would be too rough and heavy. I checked in the kindling pile, but there were no sticks straight enough."

"So what did you do?" Friend Lucretia asked.

"I saw a pair of old men's leather shoes in the corner with some clothing that had been donated to the orphanage. I asked Lionel for a knife and cut the soles of the shoes away from the rest of the shoe. It was good strong leather, and large enough to use."

"Use for what?"

"I drew a pattern using Andrew's other arm—his good arm. Then I soaked the leather in hot water to soften it and traced the pattern for the splint onto the leather. Using Lionel's knife, I carefully cut out the two splints."

"Good thinking!"

"I let the leather cool a bit to the touch, but while it was still warm and malleable, I folded it over Andrew's broken arm. One on the top, one on the bottom. Lionel helped hold Andrew, and Mrs. Whitaker held the two pieces of leather together while I cut strips of muslin from a sheet. Some of the strips I used as padding between Andrew's arm and the leather. The other strips I used to tie around the two leather splints. Not too tight to hurt, but strong enough to support his arm."

"I am impressed!"

"Thank you. Andrew whimpered, but he had stopped hollering. When Dr. Dixon arrived later that evening, he said he could not have done a better job himself."

Lucretia clipped away some more weeds from her blackberry vines. "How did thee feel when he said that?"

"I was proud and happy."

"What made thee think of the leather soles of the shoes for a splint?"

"I'm not sure. What is it they say? 'Necessity is the mother of invention.'"

"Ah, yes. An important quality for being a mother ... and for being a doctor!"

I always like being with Friend Lucretia. She seems to believe I could do or be anything I dream. No matter what the obstacles.

That night, after the wagon was loaded with flowers, chickens, eggs, and early peas, we began the drive back to the Shelter.

Zebulon was asleep in my arms within minutes of the wagon beginning its rhythmic swaying.

"He's a good boy," said Lionel.

"Yes, he is."

"Makes you wonder what kind of parents he had. To be so good, I mean."

"It seems like all the children who come to the Shelter must have a story about how they lost their parents."

"What is Zebulon's story?"

"They died. Together. Left Zebulon all alone in one night's time."

The sound of the horses' steady plodding filled the night air. We sat in silence for a while, then Lionel asked, "Do you know how they died?"

I didn't say anything at first. Then I said, "They were murdered."

"Oh my goodness, Miss Sarah. Was the boy around? Did anyone hurt him too?"

"Sometimes the hurts you get are inside ones, you know, Lionel?"

"That I do, Miss."

"Zebulon saw it. He saw the men kill his father and mother."

"How did Zebulon escape being hurt?"

"There was another man there—a good man. Zebulon's father made him promise to get Zebulon out of there. But there wasn't time for Zebulon to get away before he saw those men shoot his parents."

"And that's how he got to the Shelter?"

"More or less."

I realized I'd said enough. I had shared more of Zebulon's story than I had intended. I thought about it all the way home. Something was unsettled in my spirit. Had I said too much?

By the time we got back to the Shelter, I had convinced myself it was okay. A lot of the children at the Shelter have come from tough circumstances. I didn't say anything about slave catchers, dogs, or runaways. I didn't mention the state that this happened in. No, I'm sure I didn't say anything that would give away Zebulon's true identity.

I watched Lionel carry in the sleeping Zebulon and set him gently down on his bed. There is nothing to worry about.

Your friend,

Sarah

New York City

Fifth Month 21, 1859

Dear Sarah,

Look deep inside the pocket of this quilt square. There is a pearl that Grandfather gave me. I have always kept it with me as it reminds me of his love for me. I can think of nothing I would rather do than give it to you. Please ask your father to sell it and give the proceeds to the fund to purchase Tookie.

I have spoken with Grandfather about this. His eyes welled up with tears, and at first I thought he was disappointed with me. Then he lifted me up, twirled me around, and kissed me on the cheek. "Thee has sold the pearl of great value for something of even greater value. Thee has made me glad, Hannah Maria Brown!"

Grandfather and your uncle are hunched over drawing boards and maps all day. Grandfather is quite intrigued with the latest equipment your uncle has for surveying. I find the days long waiting for word of Pearl. The Committee knows we're staying here and will let us know as soon as they know anything.

Your friend,
Hannah

Philadelphia, Pennsylvania

FIFTH MONTH 23, 1859

Dear Hannah,

We went back to Seven Oaks today. Zebulon couldn't wait. He told Lionel that they had more "man work" to do. Lionel laughed and said, "Yes, sir, Master Zebulon. We got a heap of work to do, and we best get started."

William and Samuel were already out in the fields. I watched until Lionel and Zebulon were out of sight. I love bringing Zebulon here.

Graceanna poured me a glass of lemonade and suggested we sit out on the porch for a bit. She told me that she and William had come to a decision.

"We would love to have Zebulon be part of our family."

I threw my arms around her, nearly spilling my lemonade. "Oh, Graceanna, you could not have made me happier. I just love that little boy, and I know he is going to be so happy here."

"We want to wait to have him come live with us until the baby is born. It's only five months away."

"I understand. Can we tell him before though?"

"William and I wanted to ask him if he would like to live with us this afternoon. We need to let him know the final decision will be up to the Shelter. William has already written Mrs. Whitaker a letter for you to take back tonight."

"Graceanna, you have given me the best gift possible."

"Well, I'm counting on your offer of help!"

"Don't worry. Wild horses couldn't keep me away from here. I'll be out to visit every week. I'll keep that little Jonathan busy while you're with the baby. I'll clean, cook, whatever you need."

"Oh, I almost forgot. The Motts have a dozen chickens and bushels of early peas and beans to load up on the wagon for the orphanage. The men will be out in the fields until it's almost time for you to go. We'll need time to talk with Zebulon. Would you

mind taking the wagon down to Roadside? There will be folks there to load it up for you."

"Of course."

I was bubbling over when Friend Lucretia met me at the door.

"You'll never believe it. Guess what is going to happen today?" I spilled out everything Graceanna had just told me. My words tumbled out on top of each other. I was so eager to share the good news.

"Thy God is faithful to thee," she commented when I was done.

"So faithful. I cannot tell you how happy I am."

"Thee has no need to do so. I can see it in thy face."

At that moment, one of the men helping Mr. Mott load the wagon came inside. "Miss, we found this satchel in the wagon. Didn't want it to get chicken blood on it, so thought we'd bring it to you."

I looked at Mrs. Mott. "This isn't my satchel."

"Well, it looks like someone is going on a trip. Check inside. Maybe there will be a nameplate."

I opened the satchel. My heart went cold. Inside I saw some of Zebulon's clothes, some food, and some money. I pulled out a piece of paper. I drew in a sharp breath.

"What is it dear?"

"A notice," I said weakly.

"What does it say?"

"Reward. Three hundred fifty dollars for escaped Negro child about seven years old. Goes by the name of Zebulon Browning. Orphan child."

"Is that our Zebulon?"

"Yes," I whispered.

I dropped the flier and looked up at Friend Lucretia. "I have done a terrible thing."

"What are you talking about, child?"

"I said too much. I talked to Lionel on the way back the other night. I told him something about Zebulon. Not enough for anyone to know he was a runaway slave, but I had no idea Lionel already suspected. He'd already read this flier. He was just trying to confirm what he already thought to be true. What do I do?"

"Where is Zebulon now?"

"In the fields with William and Samuel ... and Lionel."

"Well, he's not going anywhere without this satchel. It has money in it for travel back south."

"South. Oh, Friend Lucretia, no! He can't take Zebulon back south."

"Of course not. We must make a plan."

The next thirty minutes seemed like an eternity as Friend Lucretia and I worked out what to do next.

I hugged her good-bye and drove the wagon back to Seven Oaks. I rushed in and told Graceanna what I had discovered.

"Zebulon's not safe!"

"I know. He's been identified. I've got to get him out of here."

"What should I do?"

"Call the boys in for lunch. Tell Lionel and William you will feed them later. You've got to keep the men in the field. I don't want Lionel to know what I'm doing."

When the boys came in for lunch, Graceanna prepared them a quick lunch of rolls and ham and a large mug of milk. I heard the snorting of horses and knew that it was time to leave. I hugged Graceanna.

"Don't worry," I whispered. "Just stall him as long as you can." I raised my voice and called to Zebulon. "I need you to run an errand with me!"

"Okay, Miss Sarah."

"Here," Graceanna said. "Zebulon, let me give you a hug. Samuel, come here and say good-bye to Zebulon."

"Oh, Miss Graceanna, I'll be back straightaway."

Graceanna and I looked at each other. It was all I could do not to cry.

Mr. Mott was at the door. "You need to hurry. I've put the satchel in the buggy. Here's money for the tickets. Now, go!"

I lifted Zebulon up into the buggy, flicked the reins, and urged the horses into a fast trot. It was two miles to the train station.

After a mile, I felt a darkness come over me. I sensed that

Lionel might not be far behind. I didn't know if William would be able to stop him, once Lionel realized Zebulon was gone. He'd probably unhitch one of the horses from the wagon and take off after us in a full gallop. I flicked the reins, urging the horses to a faster pace.

I looked behind me. There was another buggy bearing down on us. His horses were in a full run. It looked like he was going to run us off the road! He came up alongside me. It was Peter Pennington! Oh no! Is he in on this too? I urged the horses on faster and faster. Zebulon gripped me tightly. I kept trying to reassure him, but I knew he could tell I was scared.

Mr. Pennington caught up again beside me. He shouted, "Mrs. Whitaker sent me. Pull over."

Sure. It's just a trap.

"Lionel's a spy."

Well that much is true.

"He plans to kidnap Zebulon," he shouted. "Wants the reward money."

I flicked the reins again and pulled ahead. I had to think. I prayed. Hard. The only word that came to me is "Things are not what they seem."

What should I do? Do I trust him?

"Zebulon. Get down on the floor. Cover up with this blanket. Don't say a word. And whatever you do, do not move."

"Whoa! Whoa there!" As the horses pulled over in a lathered sweat, I jumped down from the buggy. I held the reins but stayed as far away from the buggy as I could. I didn't want Mr. Pennington to see inside.

"Why, Mr. Pennington, you scared me to death! What do you want?"

"You can't go to the railroad station."

"What?"

"That's exactly where he will look. You've got to take my buggy instead. You have Zebulon with you, right?"

I didn't say a word.

"Look, I know you don't like me. Right now, you don't trust me. I understand that. There's not much time. I was with Mrs. Whitaker earlier today, right after you left for Seven Oaks. One of the other workers there at the orphanage rushed in and told Mrs. Whitaker that Lionel had cleaned out his locker and that the cash box had been broken into. When we went to investigate, we found this." Mr. Pennington showed me the flyer about Zebulon — the same one I had found in his satchel. "Mrs. Whitaker asked me to come here as fast as I could. Lionel may be a spy. We think he's going to kidnap Zebulon and sell him back down south."

"But I've got to get Zebulon back to Philadelphia."

"I agree, but here's what we'll do. Let's switch buggies. I'll take the Motts' buggy. I'll make sure it gets back to them later. You take my buggy, but don't go to the railroad station. I'll head in that direction slowly, and let Lionel track me. I'll be the decoy."

"Where should I go?" I asked.

"You take my buggy, go as fast as you can to Philadelphia. Here, I've written out the directions. Now hurry."

"What do I do when I get there? I can't go back to the Shelter."

"Don't lose this piece of paper. Go to this address. Henrietta Duterte. She's a friend of mine. She'll figure out what to do next. Now hurry!"

We switched buggies. Mr. Pennington grabbed the satchel and helped Zebulon up into his buggy. "Godspeed, Sarah."

Zebulon and I got back to Philadelphia about dusk. I had memorized the address Mr. Pennington gave me: 200 Lombard Street.

Neither Zebulon nor I had said a word since we left Mr. Pennington. I wondered where he was and what had happened.

"Miss Sarah?"

"Yes, Zebulon?"

"What's going on?"

I laughed, and said, "Whew! Didn't we just have a big adventure!

Now we are going to find a nice lady who will help us with the next part of our adventure."

"What's her name?"

"Henrietta Duterte."

"That's a funny name."

"Yes, it is." Then we both laughed. I think we both needed to release some of the tension after being terribly frightened all day.

Here I am at night in Philadelphia in a part of the city I don't know looking for a woman I don't know recommended by a man I thought was untrustworthy. Oh, what are my parents going to say when I get home tonight? If I get home.

Mr. Pennington's directions were good. I pulled the buggy up in front of 200 Lombard Street. I wrapped the reins around a post and told Zebulon to stay in the buggy. I knocked softly. Four times.

The door opened, and I stared into the face of a Negro woman. "Yes?"

"Mr. Peter Pennington told me to come here. He said you could help."

She looked around me. "Who do you want me to help?"

"A boy. About seven. He's in trouble."

"Come in quickly, child."

I signaled to Zebulon, who had been watching the entire time from the buggy. We slipped into Mrs. Duterte's home. Her husband, a cabinetmaker, was there too.

She studied me for a few moments. "I can tell by your dress that you are a Quaker. Am I right?"

"Yes, Ma'am. I am."

"How do you know Peter?"

"I volunteer at the Shelter. He comes there a lot."

I didn't share my suspicions or my fear even now of having trusted him.

"He's a good man."

I didn't say anything in return.

"The boy here. He's a runaway?"

I didn't know what to say.

"Sarah, let me tell you what I know. You are a sixteen-year-old girl in Quaker dress here with a seven-year-old Negro boy. You volunteer at the Shelter, which often takes in runaways who have no parents. Some of these have run long distances from the deepest parts of the South. You know Peter Pennington. You are here late at night, frightened half to death. Am I right?"

I had to smile. She was exactly right.

"Now, you have a choice. Either you trust what Peter told you—that you can trust me—or you wait to decide if you can. But I imagine you know that time is not on your side. Otherwise, you would have returned this poor child to his warm bed at the Shelter tonight. Am I right?"

"Right again," I answered.

"Then?"

"Okay. I do need help." Then I told her the story of what had happened, realizing that I was filling in Zebulon at the same time. It seemed much too much for a young boy to have to handle—learning about Lionel's betrayal. I looked at him. "Zebulon, I'm so sorry."

"Miss Sarah, remember today when I told you I had man's work to do?"

"Yes."

"Well, this is man's work too."

Mrs. Duterte threw back her head and laughed. "Well, young man. After all that man's work, I bet you are hungry. Mr. Duterte here is going to take you into the kitchen and get you some supper."

When he left, I told Mrs. Duterte everything: what I knew of Zebulon's parents, how their deaths had affected him, what good news we were about to share with him, Lionel's betrayal, and how I got to her home that night.

"Do you know Mr. Purvis?"

"Yes, Ma'am, I do. He's been to our home many times."

"I'm going to have Mr. Duterte get Mr. Purvis and go tell your parents where you are. You'll need to stay with me a few days. He'll make sure it's okay with your parents. I've got a plan, but it will take a few days to get all we need ready. Besides, Zebulon will need you now more than ever."

I am going to sleep tonight in a strange home, but one I sense is safe. Zebulon is already asleep on a pallet spread out on the floor beside my bed. I wanted to stay up tonight to write you. It may be a few days before I can send this to you. I wonder what the plan will be for Zebulon?

Your friend,

Sarah

Philadelphia, Pennsylvania

FIFTH MONTH 25, 1859

Dear Hannah,

Early the next morning, while Zebulon was still sleeping, Mr. Purvis stopped by. Father was with him. I was never so glad to see Father. I hugged him tightly and broke down and cried. I felt so much better after a good cry.

"William took the train into the city last night to alert us to what had happened," he explained. "He wanted to make sure you and Zebulon made it back here all right. When he realized we hadn't heard from you, we were frantic. Bless Mr. Duterte, though. He showed up not much longer after William did and set our mind at rest. Robert Purvis was with him, and we were assured of your safety and that Zebulon was fine."

"Did William tell you what he and Graceanna decided?"

"Yes, but Sarah ..." Father paused and looked at Mr. Purvis. "It's no longer going to be safe for Zebulon here in Philadelphia, at the Shelter, or with anyone who they know cares for him. That means our family at Seven Oaks."

"No!" I started crying all over again. "No! It isn't fair! It was all going to work out. It was okay with Graceanna. I was going to help!"

"I know. Sarah, it's no longer safe for Zebulon to be here with you either. Mrs. Whitaker found out that Lionel had already alerted the slave catchers and made a plan for returning Zebulon to them. The slave catchers know about Zebulon, the Shelter, Seven Oaks, and you."

Mr. Purvis added, "To help Zebulon now, Sarah, we need to get him to Canada."

"Canada! But I'll never see him again!"

Mrs. Duterte said, "Sarah, you have done your part. You have kept Zebulon safe up till now. You need to let us get him safely to Canada."

"But you don't understand. It's all my fault. I've ruined everything. If I hadn't told Lionel what I did, he never would have

figured out that Zebulon Coleman was Zebulon Browning." I sobbed loudly. "Zebulon was going to have a family. A real family. It was perfect."

"Sarah," said Mrs. Duterte, "if you are going to be involved in this Underground Railroad business for long, you will learn that we take what we get and we work with it the best we can. Every slave we get to Canada is another nail in the coffin of the worst business in the world. Getting Zebulon to Canada and to safety, where he—and you—never have to worry again that he will be thrown back into slavery ... well, that is what I call perfect."

I wiped the tears from my face. I knew they were right, but it just seemed so unfair. In my plan, having Zebulon grow up with Samuel in a loving home was the best thing I could think of. But they were right; there was more here at stake—his safety and making sure that he never, ever, was sent back to slavery. That is what his parents wanted for him. That is what his parents sacrificed their lives for. I didn't have to like the way things were turning out, but I did need to be thankful for these wonderful people who were here now to help Zebulon.

I took a deep breath, sighed, and said, "So what's the plan?"

Father hugged me and whispered, "That's my girl."

Then Mr. Purvis and Mrs. Duterte laid out the most incredible plan I could have imagined. Step by step. In two days Zebulon would be on his way to Canada.

"Would you like to be a part of it?" she asked.

"Would I!"

I can't wait for tomorrow.

> Your friend,
> Sarah

Philadelphia, Pennsylvania

Fifth Month 26, 1859

Dear Hannah,

This morning, we rose early.

"Zebulon, I've got some very good news for you." I was so glad we had not yet told him about William and Graceanna's decision to bring him into their home. "These people want to make sure you get all the way to Canada. You've heard of Canada, right?"

His eyes shone. "Oh yes, Miss Sarah, my mammy and pappy talked about it all the time. They said that in Canada, you are free. No man can own you."

"That's right. But there are some bad people who don't want others to make it to Canada. They want to stop them."

"I heard about them too," Zebulon said solemnly.

"Sometimes people need to have a disguise to get past them. One girl we just helped is about my age, but I made her a disguise so she looked like a boy. I made her pants and a shirt and got her a cap so she could hide her hair. She had to learn to walk like a boy."

"Like this?" Zebulon swaggered around the room with his thumbs tucked in his waistband.

I laughed. "Yes, just like that."

"Did she make it to Canada?"

"Yes, she sure did. Her name is Pearl. Now we're trying to help her sister get to Canada too."

"Will I be disguised?"

"I don't know, but it will take a good plan to make sure no one can tell you are really an escaped slave. You know, Zebulon, you're not really free until you get to Canada these days."

"Will you come with me?"

I swallowed hard. I couldn't cry, not now, not in front of Zebulon. "Well, if I came to Canada, then I wouldn't be here to help other children get to Canada too, now would I?"

Zebulon thought hard for a moment, then brightened. "But you would come visit me? You and Samuel?"

"Oh, wouldn't that be wonderful?" I hadn't really answered him, but he seemed satisfied. "So do you want to hear the plan?"

I told him all the details, and he laughed and laughed. "Miss Sarah, now that is some disguise!"

Mrs. Duterte came in when she heard the laughter, and said, "Ready?"

Zebulon, still chuckling, said, "Are you the lady undertaker?"

"I am."

"Well, here I am. Better measure me for my casket." Then he burst out laughing again.

"I think the hardest part of the plan," I offered, "is going to be keeping Zebulon quiet in the casket!"

Mrs. Duterte winked. "Zebulon, you want to know what I have planned for Miss Sarah's disguise?"

His eyes grew large as she whispered it into his ear. I couldn't hear what she was saying. "Oh, Ma'am. I can't wait to see that!"

We heard the sounds of Mr. Duterte in the basement, sawing wood for Zebulon's casket. "Funeral procession begins at 3:00 p.m. today," Mrs. Duterte said. "We are going to process all the way out of Philadelphia."

"To Canada!" Zebulon proclaimed.

We spent the rest of the morning selecting proper attire for the poor deceased seven-year-old boy. Zebulon giggled through the fitting and kept saying, "Oh, Miss Sarah, you're next!"

I looked at Mrs. Duterte, but she just smiled.

After lunch, she explained to Zebulon everything that would happen. "Now it's Sarah's turn," she said.

She took me into her bedroom and selected a flowing black dress and ample petticoats. "Here, try this on." It was unlike anything I had ever worn as a Quaker. It was made of satin and silk, trimmed in ribbons, and had layers and layers of skirts. When I came out, she nodded her approval.

Zebulon said, "Now her face, Mrs. Duterte."

Mrs. Duterte pulled out a vial of silver nitrate from her dresser. "Ready to become a Negro?" she asked.

"What?"

"This will turn your face black. It won't do to have a white girl in our procession. I assume you want to stay with Zebulon as long as you can."

"Absolutely!" I sat still as she took a cotton rag and rubbed the silver nitrate all over my face. She then placed a large feathered black hat on my head, tucking my hair up inside. The wide brim covered part of my face. She handed me her looking glass.

Even Zebulon had stopped laughing. I made quite an impression as I stood up, dabbed at my eyes with my handkerchief, and wailed, "Swing low, sweet chariot, comin' for to carry me home."

In a hushed voice, Zebulon said, "Miss Sarah, you could be my mammy."

I hugged him and said, "I couldn't love you more if I were."

Mrs. Duterte said, "Time to go. Zebulon, you know what you have to do."

He ran off towards the basement ... and his casket. Suddenly, he turned, ran back to me, hugged me, and wouldn't let go.

Mrs. Duterte said, "It's time."

I pulled his arms away, knelt by his side, hugged him, and said for the last time, "I love you, Zebulon."

He whispered, "I love you too, Miss Sarah." He ran down the stairs to the basement, and I followed Mrs. Duterte. It would not be hard to pose as a mourner today. I was mourning the loss of Zebulon. A necessary loss, but a painful one nonetheless.

Mrs. Duterte led me out to the street where the mourners were gathering. She introduced me to two women who would be my companions for the processional. They were in on the secret. "My goodness," said one, "you look just like one of us."

Soon four men came out bearing a casket on their shoulders. I knew Zebulon was inside. Only if you looked very closely would

you see the small holes drilled into the sides for air. They placed the casket onto the flower-covered cart behind the buggy pulled by four horses. The driver flicked his reins, and slowly the horses moved forward.

The mourners walked alongside, singing, praying, and crying. I thought back over the last few days and the last buggy ride Zebulon and I took together. So much has happened. So much has changed. We walked for several miles, moving slowly through and out of the city. Only a few folks knew that this casket contained a little boy who was not dead, but very much alive.

By the time we got to the edge of the city, there were five mourners left. Others had only walked with us part of the way. My two companions knew the truth. I assumed the two men driving the buggy with the casket did. I didn't know about the other two mourners—a man and a woman. Did they know Zebulon was alive in that casket?

I wasn't sure what would happen next. The processional stopped at a small cemetery just outside of the city. Two men lifted the casket off the cart and placed it gently on the ground. I looked around. Who could be watching? What do we do now?

One of the men who had ridden in the buggy stepped out in a flowing preacher's robe. "Let's gather together to pray." The remaining mourners moved in closer, forming a tight circle around the casket. One of the men knelt down by the casket and began to pray in a loud, booming voice, thanking God for the short life of this young one.

He lifted the top of the casket gently, praying all the louder. Zebulon quickly climbed out and the man put his finger to his lips, signaling him to stay quiet. Never missing a beat in his prayer, he had Zebulon slip under his preacher's robe. Another man knelt and slid the top back on the casket.

The preacher said a loud and emphatic "Amen!" and walked slowly to the buggy. The mourners kept the circle tight around him in case anyone was watching. The door to the buggy opened,

and I saw a little movement, only because I was watching. Zebulon wiggled out from under the preacher's robe and into the buggy. The preacher stepped in after him.

Tonight, once safely out of the city, he would be spirited home to home, as the Underground Railroad does best, all the way to Freedom Land. As the mourners turned to leave, I whispered, "Godspeed, Zebulon."

Your friend,

Sarah

Rochester, New York

Dear Sarah,

We had been in New York City for about two weeks when Grandfather said he was taking me to lunch at Downing's Oyster House on the corner of Broad and Wall Streets. No sooner had our oyster stew arrived than a man came to our table, leaned over, and whispered into Grandfather's good ear that his package had arrived and would be waiting for him downstairs. We finished our stew and rose to leave.

Instead of exiting the restaurant normally, however, Grandfather directed me down a passage past the kitchen to steps leading to the cellar. At the bottom of the steps there was a small room. Grandfather opened the door, and Pearl was standing before me, dressed in your disguise! We hugged and chattered excitedly; all the while Grandfather was shushing us. Grandfather told me he had to discuss some matters with the Friend who had brought the message, and he would leave us to talk.

"The first part of the trip was easy," Pearl said. "Every day was a new farm or a new home. They moved me at night, about ten miles each time."

"Where did you stay?"

"It seemed like everywhere. Barns, cellars, attics. One night the family I was staying with had unexpected visitors, so they moved me outside. I hid in a hay shock in a field all night long. That was my scariest night."

"Then what?" I asked, eager to hear her story.

"Things changed when I got to New Jersey. Your grandfather was right. From New Jersey to New York City was not quite so easy." Pearl rolled her eyes. "They turned me over to a man they just called a Friend. They said it was better I didn't know his name. He was sly, that one. He was to take me cross the Raritan River on the train and into New York City."

"What did he look like?"

"Silver hair, blue eyes, seemed old, but he seemed young too. Nearly scared me to death when he told me the slave catchers had their headquarters nearby."

"Oh, no!"

"Right before we got to the train station, a man he called Thomas stopped to ask him for directions. He spoke low, but I listened hard. Turns out that ol' Blockett and some other slave catchers were on the lookout for me at the train station."

"How did they know that?" I asked.

"Master Worthy hiked up the bounty for me again and made me worth a big prize. There were flyers with a description of me plastered all over the station." Pearl shuddered dramatically. "Ol' Silver, that's what I call him, told me we'd have to go by boat instead."

"And did you?"

"No. I was just as sly as Ol' Silver and said, 'They won't be looking for this.' I showed him the disguise Sarah sewed up for me. Told him to wait a minute. Then I changed behind a tree into my disguise quick as a jackrabbit."

"Did it work?"

"Well, I shore nuff looked like a boy, but Ol' Silver wasn't satisfied. He said, 'Walk heavy, there! Lift up your head. Eyes straight ahead. Walk straight and heavy now.'"

"Then what happened?"

"When he was satisfied with me, we started out. Took the boat to Perth Amboy and then on to New York City. No one made anything of it. Ol' Silver brought me here, and that's the last I saw of him."

"Ol' Silver, heh?" said Grandfather, returning with an older couple. "He's as sly as a silver fox, now that's the truth. He's among the best we have. Thee was in good hands, Pearl." He turned to the couple. "Meet Friend Mordecai Shoemaker and his wife, Lydia. They are your companions for the next part of the journey, Pearl."

"Nice to meet you," said Friend Mordecai. "We will leave soon and take the New York Central Railroad from Forty-Second Street Station to Rochester, New York."

"You're not far from Canada then," explained his wife. "Just cross the bridge at Niagara Falls, and you'll never have to worry again if you'll be captured."

Pearl broke out in a huge grin and said, "Freedom Land!"

I helped Pearl change into the Quaker dress Friend Lydia had brought with her. This was Pearl's disguise for this part of her journey.

"Miss Hannah, here, these are yours." Pearl handed me the slate and composition book.

"No. They are yours to keep. Use them to teach your sister one day soon how to write her own name."

I did not tell her of the discouraging news that the price for Tookie had increased again, or that Master Worthy seemed intent on keeping her.

"Hurry along now," said Grandfather. "Mustn't miss the train."

"Oh, Grandfather, please let's go with them, just to the station to see them off. I'll feel so much better once I know Pearl is on that train."

I think he was as anxious as I was to see Pearl safely on the train because he quickly agreed.

At the station, Friend Mordecai bought the tickets for Rochester.

"Keep your head down," admonished Friend Lydia. Pearl was so intrigued with the train station, the people, and sounds that she was looking all around, where anyone could see her.

We took the steps down to the track for the Rochester train. Grandfather and Friend Mordecai had their heads together, and talked in low tones, while they waited for the train to arrive. Friend Lydia tied Pearl's bonnet, which had slipped onto her shoulders. I looked around the train station. That's when I spotted him. Blockett!

He hadn't seen us yet. "Hurry," I urged the others. "Get to the

other track. Quick." We split up, with Pearl and the Shoemakers in one group and Grandfather and I in another. I led the way, going up seven steps to a landing that crossed over the track and down to the other side. The Shoemakers followed with Pearl. I looked back. Blockett hadn't spotted us yet.

Once on the other side, we had a long train between Blockett and us. The sight of Blockett made my skin grow cold, and it also made me angry. I remembered how Blockett yanked at my bonnet when he thought I was Pearl. He would have yanked off my head, given the chance. He would be no kinder to Pearl if he had her in his grip. I knew then what I had to do.

I turned to Grandfather and Friend Mordecai. "I know it is your plan to take Pearl with you to Rochester, but you might as well hand Pearl over to the slave catcher if he sees you together. What is a kindly Quaker couple doing with a young Negro girl? There are lots of free Negroes in New York, but you have to admit that's an odd combination. The slave catcher will be most curious, if not suspicious. If, however, it is just Friend Lydia with Pearl and me, it will be as natural as can be—just a Quaker teacher and her pupils on a trip to the Falls."

Grandfather stooped to pick up a flyer on the ground. It was a reward for the capture of three slaves, including a girl fitting Pearl's description. He looked at me for what felt like hours.

Friend Mordecai touched Grandfather's arm. "The child is right. We may be better suited to divert Mister Blockett and keep him from boarding the train."

Grandfather crumpled up the flyer in his hand, hugged me, and said, "I will take the next train to Rochester and meet thee there."

Friend Mordecai gave the three tickets to his wife, and we quickly boarded the train. I had the utmost confidence that if anyone could divert Mister Blockett, it would be Grandfather. Even though Pearl was trembling in the seat next to me, I was certain we were safe now.

The train chugged out of the city. When the conductor came for

our tickets, he looked curiously at the three of us. I felt Pearl stiffen. I held my breath.

Friend Lydia handed him the tickets and said, "This one is for me, and these two are for my students." The conductor tipped his hat to Friend Lydia and moved on down the train. Pearl and I looked at each other. It was going to be a long train ride.

About an hour later, the car door opened and a man with a small valise took a seat facing us, a few rows away. He took out some papers from the valise and read through them. He kept looking at his papers, then at Pearl, then at the papers again. Pearl noticed and nudged me.

Friend Lydia pulled out her Bible and began to read. That gave me an idea. I said rather loudly, "Friend Lydia, is it time for our lessons?" Friend Lydia, who had not noticed this man, appeared a bit confused. "I thought Polly and I could do some copy work if you will lend us your Bible."

I nudged Pearl, who pulled out her slate and chalk from her small bag. Pearl wrote the name Polly across the top of the slate. At that moment I was so thankful that Mother had insisted I teach Pearl her alphabet during her stay at Evergreen. Even though reading was coming along slowly, Pearl could write her letters. If she could just copy down what she saw in the Bible, then that should be enough.

The man continued to stare at us. Finally he stood and walked up to our seats. He directed his comments to Friend Lydia. "Are you a teacher?"

"Why, yes, sir," replied Friend Lydia.

"And these are your students?"

"Yes. This is Hannah and this is—"

"Polly," I said quickly. I was so afraid that Friend Lydia was about to say Pearl's name.

"In the South, where I am from, it is against the law to teach reading and writing to slave children," he said coldly, looking straight at Pearl. Pearl slumped in her seat. I nudged her again hard to make her sit up straight.

"I have heard that is true," replied Friend Lydia, "but fortunately, in the fellowship of Friends we believe all should learn to read and write."

"Can this one read?" he said, pointing to Pearl.

Friend Lydia paused, not knowing what to say. I very sweetly inquired, "Would you like to hear Polly read from the Bible?" I took the Bible from my lap, turned to Psalm 23, and said to Pearl, "Here, Polly, read Psalm 23 for this man."

Pearl took my cue. Of course, I knew she had memorized this psalm long ago and could easily quote it from memory. Pearl held the Bible and pretended to read as she recited Psalm 23.

"Read something else," he demanded.

"We really must get back to our copy work."

"Sir, I must ask you to leave. You are upsetting my students." Friend Lydia rose and stepped out in the aisle, placing her body between this man and us.

Pearl looked at me and mouthed, "He knows." I could see small beads of sweat forming on her brow.

"Polly, will you hold the Bible for me while I copy the psalm? Then I'll hold it for you afterwards," I said as calmly as I could.

Pearl picked up the Bible and held it up high. She turned towards me so the Bible hid her face. If this man had taken one good look at her, her expression would have told him what he wanted to know. What if he asked her to read something else? I thought. Something that she hadn't memorized?

My hands were shaking. I could hardly hold the chalk as I wrote on the slate. I stayed focused and tried to act as if nothing was wrong.

Friend Lydia said, "Sir, I'll ask you once again. Then I shall call for the conductor. Please leave us alone."

The man shrugged his shoulders, tucked his flyers under his arm, picked up his valise, and walked to the next car. I heard him mutter as he went by, "No slave girl from Carolina can read the word of the Lord like that anyway."

Pearl said, "Did you hear that! He thought I was the escaped slave from South Carolina."

I shushed her. "Well, you are," I whispered, "but he doesn't think Polly is that person, now does he?"

Friend Lydia sat down, and the three of us tried to relax, but I kept an eye out for that man to come back the whole rest of the train ride.

When we arrived safely in Rochester, we were met by Friends

who would take us to a safe house. It was not until we were in the buggy that the three of us relaxed.

Sarah, you will never guess whose home we stayed in. Dr. Dolley ... and her husband, Dr. Dolley! They are conductors on the Underground Railroad here in Rochester!

Sarah, the most remarkable thing happened next. We were only in the Dolleys' home for a few hours when four more Negroes arrived. One of them was a fugitive slave who helps other runaways to escape. She had three passengers with her. The woman's name is Harriet Tubman. She is a most unusual person — small in stature but physically strong. Her presence seems to fill the room.

"Will you journey with us tomorrow to Canada?" Miss Tubman asked Pearl.

At the sound of the name Canada, Pearl began to cry. "My pappy's in St. Catharine's, just over Niagara Falls."

Miss Tubman placed her hands on Pearl's shoulders and looked deeply into her eyes. "I will take you to him. The Lord told me this morning that I would have another child of his to take to the Promised Land." Miss Tubman smiled. "Weep no more unless it is for joy. Your prayers for deliverance have been answered."

I have never felt the Spirit so strongly as at that moment. Neither Pearl nor I could stop the tears flowing down our faces. They were tears of joy and tears of revelation. We knew in our hearts that he had been with Pearl as she left the cotton fields of South Carolina and hid in the swamps of North Carolina. He had been with her through the chase to the Potomac River in Virginia, through the hand-off from Friend to Friend for miles and miles, on the boat in New Jersey, and on the train in New York. I know in my heart, Sarah, that he has not forgotten Tookie either.

In awe of his power, I remain your
faithful friend,
Hannah

Philadelphia, Pennsylvania

SIXTH MONTH 11, 1859

Dear Hannah,

When Master Worthy found out that Pearl had escaped Blockett again in New York City, he was furious. Apparently, two old men strong-armed Blockett into a lengthy argument while a train to Rochester left the station. Even though we raised the $3,000, he would not sell Tookie.

Today, when I was at the Shelter, Peter Pennington came to visit. It was the first time I've seen him since that night when he helped me escape with Zebulon. I rushed up to him.

"Mr. Pennington, can you ever forgive me? I misjudged you."

"I knew you didn't like me."

"Was it that obvious?"

"Yes. I was acting, and you sensed it. You thought I was lying, and I was. You thought I was a Southern sympathizer here to spy on the Shelter, and report to slave owners about runaways. In truth, however, it is the opposite. I am not a peddler by trade, but it is a good cover for my work in the South."

Mrs. Whitaker chimed in, "It is Peter who spies on the slave owners. I can't tell you the number of slaves we have been able to identify and reunite with family members who have already escaped to Canada. And it's all because of Peter." She patted his arm. "His eccentric ways and his peddler business take him inside plantations that other abolitionists, even those who pose as fellow slave owners, can't go."

"Very rewarding work," he said.

"Well, I can't believe I misjudged you. If it weren't for you, I don't know where Zebulon would be now."

"Miss Sarah, I take no offense. I've been thinking though. I might have an answer for your problem with Tookie."

I looked surprised, but Mrs. Whitaker added, "I've filled him in on everything."

"If you and the others agree, I will go to South Carolina and sell

my wares to the neighboring plantations near Oakwood. At night, I'll meet with the slaves and work with them to devise a plan to rescue Tookie. I'll bring her back with me."

"You could do that?"

"I think I can," Mr. Pennington said.

Mrs. Whitaker explained, "He's too modest. He's done it scores of times before."

"It's a bit more complicated this time," he said. "From what I understand, Tookie is tied to the bedposts in the Worthy bedchamber at night. Night is usually the best time to attempt a rescue."

"So would you rescue her in the day?" I asked.

"Oh, no, it is much too dangerous. There would be too much activity going on at the main house."

I tugged on his sleeve. "Let's go right now and meet with Father and the others. I don't want to waste another minute."

Mr. Pennington drove the buggy to my house, and Father gathered some of the Committee members to discuss the plan. Nathaniel was there and volunteered to go along to help in any way he could. He is so courageous. I never knew that before.

Father could tell I wanted to volunteer as well, but before I could even get the words out of my mouth, he said, "You have had enough excitement for one month."

It was long after midnight when the plans were finalized. The men provided money for supplies and wares for Mr. Pennington to sell. They also provided money for train tickets to North Carolina. They would stay with Friends who would supply them with a wagon and horses. They could buy the wares there in North Carolina.

Nathaniel would go along at least as far as the South Carolina border. He would wait there at a farm that was one of the stations for the Underground Railroad. When Peter returned with Tookie, there would be fresh horses ready for the journey back.

All agreed that the best route for this little girl was station to station until she reached Canada. Trains would be too closely watched by the slave catchers after Pearl escaped that way.

As everyone rose to leave, I suddenly remembered and asked everyone to wait. I raced up to my room, opened the middle drawer of the bureau, and grabbed the small metal object. I ran back downstairs.

"My friend, Hannah, gave this to me for safekeeping when she visited me." I unfolded the fabric for one of our quilt squares, and it rolled out onto the table. Not a sound could be heard except for the clink of the metal against the table.

"It was Pearl's. It was still on her neck the night she arrived at Evergreen. Hannah's grandfather cut it off that night."

Mr. Pennington grew excited. "Excellent, Sarah, excellent! This slave tag will be exactly what I need. Look everyone, see how it says Oakwood Plantation on one side, and a number. That's the number of the slave Worthy bought. He likely recorded the number in his ledger book along with a description of the slave he bought or sold, and the price paid. Sometimes house servants have their name on the tag. See here, PEARL.

"This will be most useful," Mr. Pennington said. "Most useful, indeed!"

I was glad that he was so pleased. At least I could contribute something to this venture.

The people began to leave. Soon, it was just Mr. Pennington, Nathaniel, and his parents, along with my family. "Ready, young man?" said Mr. Pennington, as he gathered the items he had received for the trip.

"Ready, sir."

Nathaniel looked at me, and I smiled at him, the kind of smile that my friends would say encourages him. He smiled back and said, "Remember us in your prayers." I assured him I would and watched as he and Mr. Pennington walked down the street to his buggy.

I can't wait to hear what happens. I wish I could go with them.

Your friend,

Sarah

Philadelphia, Pennsylvania

SIXTH MONTH 20, 1859

Dear Hannah,

Tonight, I was washing the supper dishes when there was a knock at the door. With the dishtowel in my hand, I opened the door and there stood Peter Pennington and Nathaniel!

"We came here straight away."

"Come in." I stepped back and opened the door wide. "Tell me quick, did you rescue Tookie?"

"All in good time. Gather your parents."

I ran to get them. When all were present, Mr. Pennington began.

"When we got to North Carolina, we took a day to prepare. Nathaniel readied the horses and the wagon, and we did some shopping for peddler's wares that could be sold at the plantations." He looked my way. "We picked up some yarn of many different colors, made of southern cotton, for a reasonable price. Tools, medicinal ointments and potions, and fabrics are always big sellers."

Get to the rescue, I wanted to shout, but held my tongue.

"When I got to Edisto Island, I asked about the main plantations that might be interested in my wares. Of course, Oakwood was mentioned. I got directions to each plantation. At night, I unhitched one of the horses and made my way as quietly as I could to Oakwood Plantation. I came up from the creek side, not the river, and as I suspected saw the slave cabins. I knew that often slaves hunt and fish at night for extra food, and I would likely be able to run into someone who could tell me about Tookie."

"Did you?" I blurted out.

"Sure enough, about ten o'clock that night, I ran into two men. At first they were frightened. You know, white man in the creek area with them. I'd be scared too. But when I mentioned Joseph and Pearl, and that they were in Canada, they were more than willing to listen."

"So they believed you?" I asked.

"Pearl's slave tag made all the difference. I told the men that I was there to get Tookie away and send her on the Underground Railroad up to Canada.

"The men said they had heard of this railroad and wanted to know how to get there. I told them there were many in the North who do not approve of slavery and are doing everything they can to help slaves when they escape. I explained about the stations, and how the slaves move from one home to the next until they reach Canada.

"I told them that Joseph and Pearl wanted Tookie to join them. And I was there to help. I showed them Pearl's tag and told them some of the story of how Joseph and Pearl made it to Evergreen."

"What did they say?" I asked.

"They said, 'We'll help you, but Master keeps Tookie with him at night.' So I asked if one of them could get a message to Tookie."

One of the men volunteered. "My missus works in the master's kitchen. She can tell Tookie what you wants."

"'Give her this to give to Tookie,' I said, handing him Pearl's slave tag. 'Tell her that there is a man she can trust, a white man, who will take her to her sister and father. But she has to figure out a way to get out of the house. I'll be waiting by the lower creek bed tomorrow night.'"

I interrupted. "Mr. Pennington, Tookie's only about five or six. What made you think she could figure out a way out of that house? Especially when you knew she was tied up at night."

"I've been in this business a long time. I've seen amazing things. I had no doubt that her desire to be back with her sister and her father would lead her to a plan. After all, she's the one who best knows the evening habits of the Worthys and any possible means of escape."

"So did she? Escape, I mean."

"That night I waited. Tookie didn't come. I was disappointed, but not discouraged. I'd be back the next night." Mr. Pennington nodded. "The next day, Tookie went outside to empty the chamber pot. She searched for the sharpest rock she could find and slipped it into her pocket."

"Why?" I asked.

"You'll see. That night, when she was cleaning up from dinner, she put some corn bread crumbs into her pocket. Later that evening, when she warmed the baby's milk, she took the corn bread crumbs from her pocket and some of the warm milk from the baby's bottle and mashed them together. She made a thick mush, which she fed to the baby with her fingers. The baby's tummy was so full that she slept soundly. Tookie needed that baby to sleep as long as she could before wakening, because when she did, and Tookie wasn't there to rock her back to sleep, the Master would be out like a flash with his dogs chasing after her."

I felt my heart pounding in anticipation.

"Tookie felt for the sharp-edged rock in her pocket and clenched it in her fist. She waited until Master Worthy was snoring. Then she wiggled the jagged rock back and forth, sawing through the rope that bound her to the cradle and the bed. As she slipped out the door, she whispered a silent thank you to God for the jagged piece of flint and to the master who carelessly made only one loop in the knot binding her to the bell rope that night."

"Then what happened?"

"She ran as fast as she could to the dry creek bed where I was waiting for her. She clutched Pearl's tag in her hand. I told her, 'My name is Peter Pennington, and I am a friend. Soon, you are going to be with your sister and daddy again. They are safe in Canada.' She nodded and kept looking back at the main house. I lifted her up on the horse in front of me, and we rode like the wind.

"I had left the wagon and the other horse tied to the tree a half hour outside of Edisto. We hitched the two horses to the wagon and started our journey to the state border. There Nathaniel met me with fresh horses. He took the wagon back to the farm where we had borrowed it, and I took Tookie on the back of a fresh horse to a neighboring farm to begin her journey, station to station, on the railroad that cannot be seen."

"Where do you think she is now?" I asked.

"Probably not that far from here. She should be in Canada very soon."

By this time, Nathaniel's parents and some of the other Committee members had arrived. Father had paid a messenger to tell them that the peddler had returned. Of course, Peter and Nathaniel had to tell the story all over again. I enjoyed it even more the second time I heard it!

Tookie is supposed to go to Canada by way of Rochester. We are donating the money we raised to the Committee.

Oh, how I would love to see Joseph's and Pearl's faces when their beloved Tookie is returned to them! Hearing the story of Tookie made me miss Zebulon even more. I prayed for him again tonight.

Your friend,

Sarah

Rochester, New York

SIXTH MONTH 25, 1859

Dear Sarah,

As soon as your letter arrived, I read it to Grandfather. At the end, I said, "Grandfather, I have to take Tookie to Canada."

I began my fervent list of arguments as to why this would be a wise thing to do, when Grandfather placed his finger on my lips and said, "Hush, child. Thee does not have to convince me of the rightness of the thing you desire. Thee will accompany little Talitha to Canada, and I will make the arrangements. Besides, I have never seen Niagara Falls. I should desire to see it before I see God face-to-face."

Grandfather told me that Tookie is expected in Rochester any day now. From here, the three of us will take the train to St. Catharine's, Canada. I cannot wait to meet her.

Faithfully,

Hannah

St. Catharine's, Ontario, Canada

SIXTH MONTH 28, 1859

Dear Sarah,

We waited at the train station for Tookie to arrive. Grandfather sat calmly on the bench, reading his newspaper, while I paced the platform, straining to hear a whistle or see the smoke of the coming train. "The train will be here soon, Grandfather. What if Tookie was caught? What if she doesn't get here before we're supposed to leave?"

"Thee must have faith," replied Grandfather. "The good Lord did not bring Tookie this far to abandon her. Now sit."

"I can't sit, Grandfather. I am too excited."

Grandfather rose and leaned out over the tracks to see if the train was coming around the bend. "I must admit, Hannah Maria, that I too am very excited. I have never seen Canada or Freedom Land, as Joseph likes to call it. In all these years, I have never had the chance to see what happens to these dear people when they finally reach Canada.

"I want to see their faces when they know that forever they are free. I have seen the fear, the anger, and the terror in so many eyes. The good Lord is gracious to me that I may now see the joy, the peace, and the liberty that will shine in Joseph's and Pearl's eyes as they gather up little Tookie in their arms."

"And the love," I added.

"Yes, Hannah, the love of this family is strong, and thee has been privileged to share in it."

At that moment the train whistle sounded. Billowing smoke from the engine filled the sky. I grabbed Grandfather's arm as the black locomotive chugged around the bend and headed for the station.

We scanned the passengers who gathered to board this train. No sign of Tookie. Grandfather and I walked down the platform, searching for any sign of a young girl. There was none.

"Grandfather, we only have a few minutes before the train leaves." What if something had happened to Tookie? She should

have been here by now. "What if Blockett got word that she was coming this route?"

Fears flooded my mind. My eyes darted from one man to the next to see if Blockett was here as well. Maybe Tookie was hiding because her escort had spotted Blockett. Oh, we can't have come this far only to fail now!

Suddenly, Grandfather spotted someone. "Ho ho!" he exclaimed. "What have we here? Dear Friend Eliza!"

Sarah, it was Eliza Janney, your teacher from Springdale and our neighbor from Goose Creek. She lives in Rochester now.

"Friend Yardley!" she responded as Grandfather tipped the brim of his hat. "Hannah, so good to see you." Then Friend Eliza laughed. "I can tell from your face, it is not me you desire to see." She then turned and said, "Talitha, it is all right. These people cared for your sister and your father. Come on out now from behind my skirts."

A timid but beautiful young girl shyly emerged from behind Friend Eliza.

"Tookie!" I exclaimed. At the sound of the name Pearl had given her, Tookie's face lit up. "I have so much to tell you about your sister's adventures."

I took her hand and led her to a bench, where I told her about the first night Pearl came to our home. I held her hands and told her how happy we were to see her. I told her about you, Sarah, and all the work you had done to help her be free. I wish you had been there with me to share that moment.

Grandfather and Friend Eliza visited for a few moments before Friend Eliza said good-bye to Tookie, who gave her a big hug. Grandfather, Tookie, and I boarded the train for Canada the next day.

Tookie was amazed when we crossed the bridge over the Falls, but it was Grandfather who stood there at the railroad car window with tears in his eyes. "This is the Lord at his best!" he exclaimed. "He works such wonders and then lets us share in them."

The train slowly came to a stop at the St. Catharine's station in Ontario, Canada. Grandfather scooped Tookie up in his strong arms and held her face to the window. "Freedom Land, Tookie. No more masters. No more slaves. Just you and your pappy and your sister in thy Promised Land."

Grandfather stepped down onto the platform. I was right behind. He set Tookie down gently. That's when she saw her father and Pearl standing beside him. She ran as fast as her legs could carry her and jumped up into her father's arms. Pearl laughed and cried all at the same time. Never have I seen such joy. Grandfather and I stood arm in arm, watching them. Our hearts were so full, I thought we would burst with joy ourselves.

Then Joseph put Tookie down next to Pearl and got down on his knees. Right there on the platform. Pearl and Tookie joined him. He raised his eyes to heaven, and with tears pouring down his face, he prayed, "Jesus, thank you for bringing my child to me. Thank you for bringing us to Freedom Land one by one. Thank you for keeping us safe, and thank you for Friends who showed us the way, fed and clothed us, and gave us shelter. Thank you for my children, Pearl and Tookie, and we ask your protection over William, Lord. Please, somehow, bring William to us too. Thank you for the years we had with their dear mother, who is with you. Now bind us together as a family in this Promised Land. Oh, Jesus, we thank you!"

Grandfather whispered to me, "Let's give them a little time together."

As we walked to a bench on the other side of the platform, I grinned and asked Grandfather, "How soon do you think we can get another package to deliver to this Railroad?"

Your committed friend,
Hannah

Philadelphia, Pennsylvania

SEVENTH MONTH 25, 1859

Dear Hannah,

I stopped by the Shelter today to meet the new orphan that Mrs. Whitaker wants me to work with. She's five years old and lost both her parents in a fire recently here in the city. She doesn't talk.

Mrs. Whitaker said, "I save the hard cases for you."

"I miss Zebulon," I answered. "A lot."

"I know you do. That's the hardest part of this business, being only part of their journey. But I have some news that may cheer you up."

"What is it?"

"Do you remember telling me that you shared the story of Zebulon's escape with Pearl when you saw her in New York city?"

"Yes, she couldn't believe Zebulon was spirited out of Philadelphia in a casket. And she sure couldn't picture me as a Negro!"

"She told her father the story. He got in touch with Mr. Pennington, to thank him for all he did for Tookie. That's when he told him his idea. Mr. Pennington arranged it all. Next week, Zebulon is coming to the settlement at St. Catharine's."

I looked at her, confused.

"To live with Joseph, Pearl, and Tookie! Joseph's working at a lumber mill. Now that he doesn't have to work to earn money to purchase Tookie, he told Mr. Pennington that there is plenty of room in his family for one more."

"Really?" I couldn't help clapping. "I can just imagine Zebulon and Tookie now. What a pair! I wish I could see him, but you're right, it does help to know that he will be with them."

"You helped him get his start on this new journey. They will take it from here."

"I'm so glad he'll have a family again, even though I miss him."

"Now, what about you? You'll be in your twelfth and final year this next year at Friends Central. What about your journey?"

"You mean, becoming a doctor?" I had shared with Mrs. Whitaker some of my frustrations with convincing my parents about studying medicine. "I'm not giving up, but it's much harder than I thought it would be."

"Of course, it is," said Mrs. Whitaker. "It's supposed to be that way."

I looked at her quizzically.

"If the course is too easy," she explained, "then the journey is not half as satisfying."

I didn't really understand what she meant, but I nodded as if I did.

That afternoon when I arrived home, we had guests. Friend Lucretia was in our parlor with another woman, talking with my parents. I greeted Friend Lucretia, and she said, "Sarah, I would like thee to meet a good friend of mine, Dr. Ann Preston."

I shook her hand, but you can imagine what my mind was thinking. Here is Friend Lucretia, with a woman doctor, in my home with my parents who are dead set against my being a doctor. Oh, how I wish I had been here sooner. I would have loved to listen in on this conversation!

Mother said, "Did you know that the Motts helped fund the Female Medical College?"

No, I did not! Friend Lucretia had never said a word to me about it, even though we'd often talked about my desire to attend there.

"Dr. Preston is Professor of Physiology and Hygiene at the college," explained Friend Lucretia.

"Sarah," Dr. Preston said, "I am pleased to meet you. I understand you have been a bit frustrated at the lack of opportunity to learn physiology in your high school."

"This year the Boys' School will have classes," I explained, "but the girls are not permitted to attend. We have to learn astronomy instead."

"Someday that will change. But in the meantime, what do you plan to do about it?"

I was uncomfortable. It had been so long since I had talked to

Father and Mother about this. My work at the Shelter, our plans for Pearl and Tookie, helping Zebulon, and my regular schoolwork had taken so much of my attention. I wondered what my parents were thinking about this conversation happening right here in their home.

I looked at them and gulped. "Well, Nathaniel, he's a friend of mine in the Boys' School. He said he would loan me his physiology book."

Dr. Preston frowned slightly. "But who will teach you? Who will explain the textbook to you? Who will direct your experiments?"

"I didn't think about that. I assumed I could learn it on my own. Or perhaps Nathaniel would share his class notes with me and tutor me."

"Or perhaps I could tutor you," said Dr. Preston. "Once a week. At the Medical College."

I could not believe what I was hearing. I shook my head. "Did you say you would teach me?"

"It would be a privilege to do so."

Friend Lucretia nodded at me, and said, "Thy parents. Why don't you ask them what they think?"

Tentatively, I looked at Father and Mother. I was afraid to ask them. I was so close to having a dream fulfilled, and I wanted to savor it. I didn't want to experience the disappointment again.

Father cleared his throat. "Friend Lucretia is a strong advocate for you, and for the Medical College. She said you will have a long road ahead of you. Finishing high school, apprenticing for a year with a doctor, then medical college, and then internship at a hospital. She explained that there are just a handful of women doctors now in America and that your journey would be difficult, challenging, and costly."

I didn't know what to say. He sounded so negative, and yet …

"Your mother and I have talked. We watched you this year take on challenges we would not have handled half as well when we were your age. God has given you a keen mind. Who are we to lock it up when it has such a desire to soar?" He paused. "If you would like to study with Dr. Preston, you have our blessing."

I rushed over to them and threw my arms around them. "Thank you! Thank you for believing in me."

Then Mother added, "There is a gift from me in the spare room, the room we use for our special guests on their way to freedom. I just hope the gift doesn't unnerve them the way it does me."

I looked at Friend Lucretia and Dr. Preston. "May I?"

"Certainly," responded Friend Lucretia.

I took the stairs two at a time and lit the lamp in the room. As the wick gained strength, I saw it. Friend Bones was hanging from a pole in the corner. A desk had been placed nearby and it was covered in books—medical books.

I looked back at Friend Bones. Hannah, I do believe he was smiling at me.

Your friend,

Sarah

Epilogue

The mid-nineteenth century was a time of great social change in America, both for women and for African Americans. Taking a stand for justice and righteousness often involved great sacrifice and personal risk. In times such as these, it is often one's faith that undergirds decisions for action and provides the sustaining grace needed to face seemingly impossible challenges.

Yardley Taylor

Yardley Taylor, horticulturalist, mapmaker, geologist, and abolitionist, was affectionately known as the "Thomas Jefferson of Loudoun County." He lived in the Quaker village of Goose Creek, Virginia, on a large tract of land known as Evergreen.

In 1824, the Goose Creek Quakers formed the Loudoun Manumission and Emigration Society. With Yardley Taylor as president, the society dedicated itself "to expose the evils which result from the existence of African slavery" and argued that slavery was "entirely inconsistent with the principles of a republican government." It urged others to recognize that "slavery cannot be justified; that it is a pernicious and dangerous evil."

In 1827, the Loudoun Manumission and Emigration Society hosted the first annual Virginia Convention for the Abolition of Slavery at Goose Creek. Yardley Taylor helped draft its constitution and served as one of five executive members.

Much of his work on the Underground Railroad was not publicized, however, as secrecy was essential to assisting fugitive slaves in the largest slave-owning state in the Union. That is, until he was named in an 1858 broadside as the chief abolitionist of Loudoun County and operator of a station on the Underground Railroad at his home. Newspapers in nearby counties reported that it was widely known among the sheriffs that if a runaway slave made it to Evergreen, then he would make it to freedom.

Lucretia Mott

Lucretia Mott formed the Philadelphia Female Anti-Slavery Society in 1833 and was a delegate to the first World's Anti-Slavery Convention held in London in 1840. From the beginning, she insisted that African American and white abolitionist women work together. That commitment was tested in May 1838, during the Convention of Anti-Slavery Women held at Philadelphia Hall, the newly built headquarters for the anti-slavery society. During the speeches by the women, a mob began to hurl rocks through the windows, then brickbats. The women barely made it out in time before the hall caught fire at the hands of the angry mob.

While the fire raged, Robert Purvis smuggled key abolitionists out of the city. The final session was to be held by the women the next morning. They linked arms, black and white, and marched two by two through the heckling crowd to another location. There they adopted a resolution that read:

Resolved, that prejudice against color is the very spirit of slavery. It is, therefore, the duty of abolitionists to identify themselves with these oppressed Americans, by sitting with them in places of worship, by appearing with them in our streets, by giving them our countenance in steamboats and stages, by visiting them at their homes and encouraging them to visit us, receiving them as we do our white fellow citizens.

Lucretia Mott's commitment to the precept that all men were created equal, regardless of gender or race, was carried out in everything she did, from her abolitionist activities through her campaign for the right of women to vote. She believed that faith, connected to action, was required for substantial change.

In encouraging others to stand up against the social injustices of her day, regardless of the personal cost, she said, "I believe it to be high time there was more Christian boldness, more moral courage, amongst mankind to speak to the sentiment of their hearts, whether they be in accordance with the popular doctrines of their day or not."

Association for the Care of Colored Orphans

Founded by Philadelphia Quaker women in 1822, the Association for the Care of Colored Orphans, also known as "the Shelter," cared

for both boys and girls, ages eighteen months to nine years old. At age nine, they were established in an apprenticeship to learn a trade until age eighteen. In May 1838, after an angry mob burned down Pennsylvania Hall, it also set fire to the Shelter. Fortunately, only property, and not lives of children, was lost. In 1915, the Shelter served only girls, and later teenage girls. The Shelter continued to serve the needs of young people who needed a home until 1981.

Female Medical College of Pennsylvania

Until the mid-nineteenth century, the field of medicine was closed to women. In 1850, Quakers established the world's first medical school for women, the Female Medical College of Pennsylvania (1850–1867), which later became the Woman's Medical College of Pennsylvania (1867–1970) and then the Medical College of Pennsylvania (1970–1995).

The Female Medical College graduated its first class of eight women doctors in 1851. Dr. Ann Preston (1851) was appointed Professor of Physiology and Hygiene of the college two years later. In 1866, she became its dean, becoming the first woman dean of a medical school in the United States.

Dr. Sarah Adamson Dolley became the second woman in the world to receive a medical degree in February 1851 (Central Medical College, Syracuse, New York). In May of that year, she became the first female intern in the United States, interning at the Blockley Hospital in Philadelphia. She was a lecturer in obstetrics at the Female Medical College (then named Women's Medical College) in 1873–74. She practiced medicine until 1900 when, at the age of 70, she decided to retire. She and her husband, also a doctor, were conductors on the Underground Railroad in Rochester, New York.

Dr. Rebecca J. Cole, the second African American woman to earn her medical degree, graduated in 1866, and worked under Dr. Elizabeth Blackwell (the first woman doctor) at the New York Infirmary for Women and Children. There she gained valuable

clinical experience and developed medical strategies to deal with poverty and urban overcrowding. In 1873, she founded and operated the Woman's Directory in Philadelphia, which offered medical legal aid to women.

Dr. Susan LaFlesche Picotte, the first Native American woman doctor, graduated in 1889. She was responsible for the health care of Native Americans in Omaha. She was appointed a missionary to her tribe by the Presbyterian Board of Home Missions. She also lobbied Congress for prohibition of alcohol on reservations. In 1913, two years before her death, she saw the fulfillment of a lifelong dream, the opening of a hospital in Walthill, Nebraska, now named the Dr. Susan LaFlesche Picotte Memorial Hospital.

By the end of the nineteenth century, female physicians were approximately 5 percent of all physicians, a figure that remained the same until the 1960s. Today women comprise 24 percent of all physicians in the United States, and make up 50 percent of all those applying to medical schools.

Now the Lord is Spirit; and where the spirit of the Lord is, there is liberty.
2 Corinthians 3:17

Dear Reader,

In 1955, Catherine Marshall bought Evergreen as a home for her parents, John and Leonora Wood. You may have heard of Leonora Wood as the real-life heroine of Catherine's beloved novel, *Christy.*

Leonora treasured Evergreen—its creeks and gardens, its old trees and mysteries. She took notes of what those in the community told her about Evergreen, about Yardley Taylor, his nursery, the plants and trees, and the Underground Railroad.

When I joined the family in 1986 as the wife of Jeff LeSourd, the family's love of Evergreen became mine as well. To love Evergreen is to love its history and its people, especially Yardley Taylor, and the history of the Goose Creek community and its commitment to the abolition of slavery.

In the 1860 presidential election, Virginia omitted Abraham Lincoln from the ballot. Nonetheless, he received eleven write-in votes from Loudoun County, nine of which were from Goose Creek. Several years later, Goose Creek changed its name to Lincoln.

To prepare for this book, I researched newspaper articles, broadsides, articles, the Goose Creek meeting records, and documents to learn as much as I could about Yardley Taylor. I visited Philadelphia, stood where Lucretia Mott preached, and read her original writings. I read thousands of pages of slave narratives where men and women tell their own stories of their experiences of slavery.

I wrote this book here at Evergreen where I now live with my husband and our two teenagers, Luke and Cate. I could almost feel the land speaking to me. *Tell the stories. Tell the stories of a thousand Josephs, Pearls, Tookies, and Zebulons.* Although slavery has been abolished, trafficking in humans, 80 percent of whom are women and girls, is still a serious worldwide problem today.

The need for wisdom, faith, and courage to speak out and challenge injustice is just as strong as it was 150 years ago. My prayer is that perhaps you too will consider how you can change your world.

Your friend,

Nancy LeSourd

Quaker Silhouette
Pictures like this cut from paper were
popular in the nineteenth century.

Friendship Quilt

Lucretia Mott

Roadside

Courtesy, Loudoun Museum, Leesburg, Virginia

Yardley Taylor

Evergreen Farm, Lincoln, Virginia

Evergreen

Female Medical College of Pennsylvania

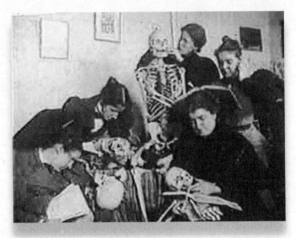

Students study the body's skeletal structure.

**Dr. Ann Preston
(1851)**

*First woman dean
of a medical school*

**Dr. Rebecca J. Cole
(1866)**

*Second African
American Woman
Doctor*

**Dr. Susan La Flesche
Picotte
(1889)**

*First Native
American Woman
Doctor*

Underground Railroad Routes 1860

Map from *The Underground Railroad* by Raymond Bial; Houghton Mifflin Company

Underground Railroad Map

The Underground Railroad had many routes north to freedom. After the Fugitive Slave Act of 1850, freedom often meant Canada.

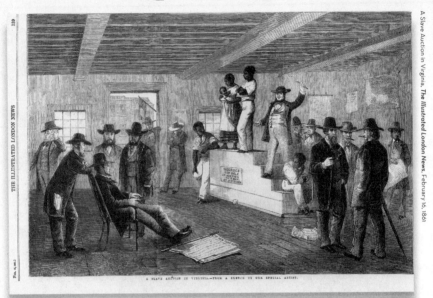

A SLAVE AUCTION IN VIRGINIA.—FROM A SKETCH BY OUR SPECIAL ARTIST.

Slave Auction

After the Sale

Slave traders strike their deals, money changes hands, and families are separated forever.

A Ride for Liberty – The Fugitive Slaves by Eastman Johnson, ca 1862; Brooklyn Museum of Art

Ride to Liberty

This painting shows a slave family escaping together. It was rare, however, for an entire family to escape at the same time.

FREE!

Liberty Letters

Secrets of Civil War Spies

 kidz

Nancy LeSourd

Richmond, Virginia

JUNE 17, 1861

Dear Emma,

I couldn't believe my eyes. "Private Franklin Thompson, of the Second Michigan Volunteers," you said. "Requesting donations for the Union Army, ma'am."

While Great Auntie Belle scurried around, loading my arms with linens, food, and medicines, so many questions swirled around in my head. How did you get to Michigan? And what, pray tell, possessed you to enlist in the Union Army? As you carried the supplies outside to the ambulance, I barely heard you whisper, "You'll keep my secret, won't you?"

"Such a nice young man, Mollie," Great Auntie commented, arms filled with more donations.

Young man? This is no man—this is Emma! I thought. *Emma, my good friend.* Last summer I was shocked when you confided in me that you left Canada with your mother's blessing to escape your cruel father. You even fooled everyone in New England, selling books disguised as a boy—one of Mr. Hurlburt's finest door-to-door salesmen. But this? A soldier in the war? Really, Emma! You've gone too far!

Your friend,

Mollie

Washington, D.C.

JUNE 22, 1861

Dear Mollie,

I know I need to explain. When Mr. Hurlburt offered me the chance to work in Flint, Michigan, I jumped at the chance to see more of this adopted country of mine. Mollie, I had to keep up my disguise. After all, I had to make a living.

Then I heard the newsboy cry out, "Fall of Fort Sumter —President's Proclamation—Call for 75,000 men!" It's true I'm not an American. When President Lincoln called for men to fight for my adopted country, I couldn't turn away. I had to help free the slaves. After much prayer, I knew God meant for me to enlist in the Army. So when my friends volunteered for the Second Regiment of the Michigan Volunteer Infantry, I assumed God would make a way for me too. But I missed the height requirement by two inches.

The day my friends left, the people of Flint cheered them on. The boys lined up with their bright bayonets flashing in the morning sunlight. Almost every family had a father, husband, son, or brother in that band of soldiers. The pastor preached a sermon and presented a New Testament to each one. Then as the bands played the "Star-Spangled Banner," the soldiers marched off to Washington. Oh, how I wanted to be with them!

A few weeks later, who should return to Flint, but my old friend from church, William Morse, now *Captain* William Morse who came back to recruit more soldiers for his regiment. This time I was ready. I stuffed my shoes with paper and stood as tall as I could. It worked! I was now Private Franklin Thompson of Company F of the Second Michigan Volunteer Infantry of the United States Army.

When I got to Washington, the army assigned me to be a field nurse. All the field nurses are men, and it doesn't matter if you don't have any training as a nurse. They tell us we'll learn it all from the field surgeons as we go. I reported to the Surgeon in charge and received my first order to visit the temporary hospitals set up all over the city. Although there are no battle injuries yet, many are sick with typhoid and malaria. There are not enough beds for the sick; not enough doctors to treat them; and not enough medicines and food.

That's why some of us decided to visit the good ladies of Washington and plead with them to donate to the Union. That was the day I saw you again — a most fortunate day for me. I hope you feel the same.

Your friend,

Private Frank Thompson, Company F,

Second Michigan Regiment

(Emma)

Richmond, Virginia

JUNE 28, 1861

Dear Emma,

Of course, I was glad to see you again, but just how do you think you can pull this off—being a private in the United States Army? Sure you can handle nursing duties. But what about shooting and riding a horse, marching and drilling, standing guard and picket duty? Can you keep your secret much longer?

Great Auntie has arranged for our letters to get to each other through her private courier now that the federal government has suspended mail to the Southern states. She is delighted I want to write to a Federal soldier. I'll address your letters to Frank so there is no suspicion. Is it all right to call you Emma in the letter? I don't want to give you away.

Great Auntie makes no secret of her support of the North, as you saw from her willingness to part with supplies for the Union. To the great embarrassment of my Richmond kin, Great Uncle Chester is now a surgeon with the Union Army and Great Auntie Belle is an outspoken supporter of President Lincoln. If Daddy were still alive, I'm sure he would agree. At least that's what I think. Momma seems to think differently.

When Momma and I arrived at Mrs. Whitfield's home today to sew uniforms for the soldiers, we heard angry voices before we even entered the room. Mrs. Whitfield told the ladies she had personally delivered a handwritten invitation to Miss Elizabeth Van Lew and her mother to join us to sew for the Confederate soldiers, but the Van Lews refused to come.

"Let's not forget they sent their daughter, Betty, to that Quaker school in Philadelphia," an outraged Mrs. Morris reminded everyone. "They filled that child's head with abolition talk, and it changed her forever."

"That they did," Mrs. Forrest agreed. "And when Mr. Van Lew died, Betty talked her mother into freeing all their slaves."

Aunt Lydia added, "I heard they even sent one of their slave girls up north to Philadelphia for her schooling and paid for it all!"

I watched the ladies ram their needles through the flannel shirts they were stitching with as much force as the words they were speaking. Personally, I think these ladies are petty gossips. So what if Miss Van Lew believes what the Union does? Is that a crime? It seems so. If they only knew what I believed, they would not permit me in their company. A Southern girl with Northern thoughts. I kept my head down as these ladies spoke. I didn't want them to see the fire in my eyes.

I excused myself as soon as I could and slipped out without much notice. No one pays much attention to a sixteen-year-old girl these days. The women worry about their boys and men and speak endlessly of the impending battles. Their attention is not on the comings and goings of someone like me.

I took this package to the place the courier designated to drop off our letters. I may have knitted for the Confederates today, but this pair of socks is included for you, my adventurous Union friend. Perhaps they will keep your feet from blistering on those long marches.

Your friend,

Mollie

Washington, D.C.

JULY 1, 1861

Dear Mollie,

Thanks for thinking about how to protect my secret. To tell the truth, I like reading my name again. To these men, I am just Frank, but to you, my good friend, I am Emma. I keep your letters tucked inside my shirt so no one can read them. I suppose for now, though, you should continue to address your letters to Frank, but just call me E in the letter. If I should lose a letter, I don't want to risk being found out.

As for riding a horse or shooting a gun, what do you think I did all those years when I was growing up on our farm in New Brunswick, Canada? I can outride and outshoot most anyone—thank you, Miss Mollie. If God has called me to this, then he has prepared me and equipped me to do what I must do. Farming was no harder work. Just try chopping and clearing the land some time, Mollie. Why, you should have seen me swing my ax to hew beams from timber as fast as the next boy. No sirree, if I'm found out, it will not be because I failed to hold my own with these brave men.

Washington is overrun with soldiers. White tents dot the landscape all around the city. The Capitol and the White House shelter hundreds of soldiers, who sit around playing cards and wait for action. Thousands of soldiers drill in the streets. Blasts from bugles and the rat-tat-tat of drums fill the air. All are eager to fight. The rebellion should be put down quickly.

Your friend,

Emma

Richmond, Virginia

JULY 4, 1861

Dear Emma,

Richmond celebrated Independence Day today, but I had to wonder, is it independence from England years ago or independence from the North it celebrates? Sissy asked me to go with her today to the camps outside the city to watch the soldiers drill. She may be two years older than I, but she has such romantic notions about this war. She thinks she can send her Lemuel off to war and he will return to her a hero. Our friends ride out to the camps every day. They dress up, bring their picnic foods, and wait for the drills to end so they can socialize with the soldiers. It all seems so silly to me — this partying with soldiers. Soldiers and girls alike think we will simply wallop the North in one big battle, and then it'll all be over. I'm not so sure.

I don't agree with you that this will be a short war. You think the boys in blue will crush the boys in gray. But here in Richmond, we too have white tents dotting the landscape like snow. Our soldiers march day and night, eager to meet the enemy. We too have hundreds, if not thousands, of young men who are certain we will capture Washington and take over the White House and Capitol where your soldiers now lounge. I do not think victory will come so easily, my dear friend, not to either side.

As the South Carolina regiment marched past us, the girls waved their handkerchiefs and cheered. They debated which regiment is the most handsome. The general consensus of our friends is that the boys from South Carolina are definitely the best looking, although the Texas regiment is a close runner-up with their rugged good looks. You see how deep their thoughts go about this war, Emma. Skin deep.

My attention was on two women handing out food and flowers to the South Carolinians. A murmur spread through the crowd. It was Miss Van Lew and her mother who smiled as they handed out their gifts. Miss Van Lew called out, "May God grant victory to the righteous!" Very clever. She didn't say which side is righteous! But the boys seemed to enjoy her attentions just the same. The women who whispered behind their fans as they watched certainly were wondering why a supposed Yankee loyalist brings food to the Confederate soldiers!

Great Auntie wrote that I can't return to Mrs. Pegram's school next fall. For the past two years since Daddy died, the Greats (that's what I call them) have paid for my education. Mrs. Pegram, with three sons fighting for the South, returned their money, and told them that Federal dollars are worthless to purchase an education for a Confederate girl. She said they could exchange their money for Confederate scrip and resend the funds for my semester's tuition.

Of course, that made the Greats furious. As much as they value my education, they won't put it ahead of their beliefs. Great Auntie prepared a box of books from Great Uncle Chester's library and sent them to me to study on my own. It's not the same though. This war is turning everything upside down.

My good friend Charlie brought the newspapers tonight and tried to cheer me up. The Confederates captured the Union steamer, the *St. Nicholas*. The paper reported that Madame LaForce—an outrageously dressed, veiled lady—boarded at Baltimore with great fanfare and seven dress trunks. Madame LaForce flirted with the sailors in French and English, but you should have seen her later when she pulled pistols and swords, not dresses, out of those trunks. Madame LaForce was really Colonel Thomas! "She" created such a distraction that no one noticed the eight men who boarded the *St. Nicholas* at Port Comfort that day and then joined Colonel Thomas in the attack on the ship that night. Later, the *St. Nicholas* captured several other Union ships filled with supplies that can now go to the Confederate Army.

My good friend Emma posing as a Union soldier, and a Confederate colonel posing as a lady. All is definitely not what it first appears!

Your friend,

Mollie

Richmond, Virginia

July 7, 1861

Dear E,

I just got your most recent letter and will do as you suggest. I want to do all I can to help you keep this secret.

Yesterday Sissy married Lemuel Hastings. And today he enlisted in the Army of the Confederate States of America. Sissy is determined to follow him wherever he is sent to fight. Momma told Sissy that her place is in Richmond with the ladies, sewing uniforms, knitting socks, and rolling bandages. Sissy bounced out of the room with her skirts swishing behind her as she tossed her head full of blonde curls. "I shall follow Lemuel to the ends of the earth," she called back to us over her shoulder. "It is my wifely duty."

Sissy has always been impulsive, but she gave Momma only three days to pull together a wedding. Even with the help of Momma's kin and their servants, there was hardly enough time to decorate the parlor, bake and display the cakes and sweets, and deliver all the invitations. Sissy decided there should be no wedding gifts. Not that anyone has any money to spare right now, anyway. In her usual fashion, she turned that all to her advantage. In her noblest of voices, she announced to one and all that they should each bring a necessity for the Confederate soldiers and deposit it in the box by the front door.

I honestly don't believe that Sissy understands what this is all about. Ever since Daddy died, it's like Sissy refuses to grow up. She'd rather pretend nothing is wrong than face facts. That's how she is with Lem and this war. She probably thinks she will pull on her white kidskin gloves, button up her dainty shoes, and swirl her hooped skirt around her as she travels by train or coach to the nearest town where Lemuel's unit is stationed. Then when he is off duty, they will dance the night away at the local town hall.

Your friend,

Mollie

Richmond, Virginia

July 10, 1861

Dear E,

Sissy and I walked to Pizzini's for ice cream. With each bite, Sissy complained about the Union blockade of our ports. If it succeeds, we will be unable to get the necessities of life. To Sissy, this means her tea and sweets. She hoards sugar in a tin can in her room. She says she may have to suffer many things in this war, but she will not suffer the loss of her sugar.

Sissy says she wants this silly war to get started so those horrible Yanks can be put in their place and her dear Lem can come home to her. I suppose that's what you are to most of those I know here: a horrible Yank.

The Northern papers Great Auntie sent me urge you Federals to stop the "Rebel Congress" from meeting here next week. "Forward to Richmond! On to Richmond! The Rebel Congress shall not meet." I admit I'm frightened. Momma too. She speaks in hushed tones with the Richmond kin. They are especially quiet around Sissy. They don't want her to be frightened for Lemuel. But how can she not be frightened? Won't he be one of the ones defending our dear city?

Will you be the one attacking it? I do not like this at all.

Your friend,

Mollie

Richmond, Virginia

July 17, 1861

Dear E,

Just three days until the Confederate government meets here. People talk quietly, especially when there are children in the room. It's not like they don't notice. The adults pretend we're safe in our homes, but you can hear the sounds of the guns and drummers on the battlefields not that far away. Sissy sits at the window, twisting her handkerchief first one way then the other. Momma told her to knit to keep her fingers busy. Sissy tried, but gave up in frustration, dropping more stitches than she could keep on the needles.

I suggested a walk. Old men spoke in hushed tones in doorways. Women whispered to one another behind fans. Only the youngest children seemed carefree. Would the Union win and be "On to Richmond"? What about the dozens of fathers, husbands, brothers, and sons that enlisted? Would they return?

Tonight Momma and the Richmond ladies gathered at Aunt Lydia's home to roll bandages and pick lint for packing wounds. Momma asked Sissy and me to come with her. I wish we were knitting socks and sewing uniform shirts. I don't like preparing for wounds and cuts and bloody bodies. I shudder to think of it. Sissy tries to join in, but I can see on her face she is wondering if the bandage she rolls tonight will be on her husband tomorrow.

Your friend,

Mollie

Liberty Letters

Attack at Pearl Harbor

Nancy LeSourd

Somewhere Over the Pacific Ocean

OCTOBER 25, 1940

Dear Catherine,

Mother always says my big mouth gets me into trouble. But today it got me into the cockpit of a Clipper Ship!

Granddaddy insisted we take the Pan Am Clipper for the last part of our trip from San Francisco to Pearl Harbor. When Mother said it was too expensive, he said we'll use military vehicles for the rest of our lives. He wanted us to have this once-in-a-lifetime experience.

But that's just it. If this is the only time I'm on a flying airship, I've got to truly experience it. That's where an eight-year-old brother who can't sit still comes in handy. I told Mother I'd watch Gordon while he went to explore. Mother leaned back, closed her eyes, and murmured, "Uh huh," which I took to mean yes.

Gordo has no clue how lucky we are to fly on a Clipper Ship. This flying ship can land on water, has places for us to sleep, and makes it possible to cross oceans in days instead of weeks. Gordo wanted to find out if a celebrity was in the deluxe cabin, but I was tired of the passenger deck. We'd already spent a lot of time here. I tugged at my dress, which had wrinkled dreadfully. I'd have to change for dinner, for sure. We've eaten all our meals in the elegant dining room with its starched white tablecloths, gleaming china and crystal, and sterling silverware. Mother insisted we dress to match. I think it's stupid to wear my white gloves to dinner, just to take them off, and try not to get any food on them.

As we walked along the passenger deck, we kept bumping into stewards wanting to fulfill my every need. "Juice, Miss Lyons?" "Another blanket, Miss Lyons?" "Care for tea, Miss Lyons?" Very annoying. What I wanted to see was the cockpit, but I didn't dare ask the steward for that. After poking around the deluxe cabin and finding no sign of a Hollywood star, Gordo was finally willing to go upstairs to the crew deck.

A small sign said "Personnel Only," but I pretended I didn't see it. While the stewards were busy, we crept up the staircase. Gordo was drawn to chocolate chip cookie smells coming from the kitchen (they call it a galley), but I pulled him on down the hall. We inched past a room where a crew member sorted mail into three different mailbags Gordo's size. The door next to the mail room flung open. We hid in its shadow as a uniformed man with papers folded under his arm marched down the hall. The sign on the door said "Navigation."

"He's headed to the cockpit," I whispered. "Let's follow him."

"Are you crazy?" Gordo said. "They're gonna kick us out of here."

"Thousands of feet above the Pacific Ocean? I don't think so. But if you're scared, go back downstairs to Mother."

Gordo shook his head, but stayed behind me as I walked toward the cockpit. We slipped by the mail room and the kitchen. The cook sang at the top of his lungs while he banged pots and pans. Gordo started giggling. I elbowed him hard, for we were right outside the cockpit door. I heard voices inside that door. "What ya gonna do now?" whispered Gordo.

The door handle turned, and I held my breath. A uniformed man stepped out of the cockpit. "Well, well, what do we have here?"

Gordo shrank back behind me. I put out my gloved hand. "Hello, sir, I'm Meredith Lyons."

"Pleased to meet you, Miss Lyons, and you too, young Master Lyons, I assume?" Gordo nodded. "Hmm ... A bit off course, are you? The stairs to the passenger deck are right over there."

Gordo started toward the stairs, and I yanked him back. "Sir, I wondered if we could see the cockpit? We've never been on an airship before."

"Not really allowed, young lady, but I'll check with the captain." He disappeared back into the cockpit. A few minutes later, he cracked the door and said, "Sorry, but you'll have to return to the passenger deck."

I stepped forward and put my foot right inside the door so that the officer couldn't shut it. He looked annoyed, but I was

determined to get inside. "Sir, you see, my whole life I've wanted to see inside a cockpit. I keep a scrapbook of all these articles about flying and planes and Amelia Earhart and everything. Sir, did you know, not too long ago, she took a photograph of a Clipper flying to California while she was flying her plane to Honolulu? Isn't that something! This might even be the exact same plane Amelia Earhart took a picture of! Everyone's been so nice down below, but it's what you important men do up here that really interests me. Please, sir. Won't you ask one more time?"

Gordo looked like he was going to die and begged me to leave before the man came back. I told him, "No way."

It seemed like an hour, but finally the officer opened the door, and said, "After you, Miss Lyons." I pushed by Gordo to get inside before the officer changed his mind.

The captain checked the dials and instruments in front of him. The other pilot scribbled something in a large brown logbook. Numbers, I think. The navigator scooted over and let Gordo sit next to him. The copilot stood up, and pointing to his seat, said, "Miss Lyons?"

As I slipped into the seat, I stared at the vast expanse of sky before me. The stars lit up the inky darkness surrounding the plane. After a few minutes, the copilot asked me what I thought. I blinked hard. The stars were still there. Without taking my eyes off the window, I whispered, "Thank you."

Back downstairs in our seats, Gordo went on and on about what he'd seen in the cockpit. Mother was furious at me. "Young lady, your father and I try to teach you what's right and proper, but you constantly amaze me. How dare you bother those pilots while they're doing their job? You know better. And to get Gordon caught up in your scheme too. Won't you ever learn?" I stared out the window and tried to block it all out. This wasn't a good time to bring up my wanting to learn to fly again. I heard Mother's voice in my head. "Absolutely not. It's simply not an option." We'd been through this a million times before over the last few years.

No, not even today on my birthday would this be a good topic of conversation.

I apologized to Mother for bothering the pilots, being a bad example for Gordo, embarrassing her, and not conducting myself as the daughter of a Naval officer. I said all the right things, but inside I was glad I'd done it. I'll never forget turning sixteen. Somehow, some way, before I turn seventeen, I'll find a way to fly.

Maybe this new assignment to Pearl Harbor will be the start of something new. After all, they call Hawaii "paradise," and what would be more heavenly than taking off into the skies, circling the clouds, and landing again—all by myself.

Your high-flying friend,

Merrie

Norfolk, Virginia

NOVEMBER 1, 1940

Dear Merrie,

I've missed you! Norfolk's not the same without you. Guess what? Dad got transfer orders to the Naval Air Station at Kaneohe. We're coming to Hawaii too!

Mom makes lists and posts them everywhere—the bathroom mirror, the refrigerator, the car dashboard. Mom and Dad talk late at night. There's much to do to get Dad ready to go, and with Hank and all, it's a challenge.

When I visited Hank today, Nurse Reynolds told me the Naval Hospital's right on the water. I can picture my brother with a bed next to a large window so he can see the palm trees and feel the warm breezes. It might make up for these horrid six months in the iron lung.

Standing next to Hank's head and talking to him, I try to block out the sounds of the iron prison he's been in for these last six months. Every day I've visited him, I've hated that machine, even though it helps him breathe as it pushes and pulls the air in his chest.

I remember listening to the radio with Hank a few months ago, when Sea Biscuit set that new track record. Hank shouted as loud as he could when the machine would let him speak. Whoosh-whooo. "Go, Biscuit!" Whoosh-whoo. "You can—" Whoosh-whoo "—do it, boy." The announcer said this patched-up crippled horse roared to the finish line in the last stretch of the race. I could see in Hank's eyes that he wants to be just like Biscuit—a down-and-out, "patched-up cripple" who astonishes people with what he can do. Hank's determined to walk again, but his determination breaks my heart. I feel so guilty keeping the truth from him, but I don't have the nerve to tell him what the doctors told us.

You remember what a great baseball player Hank was before he

got polio—especially last year on his seventh-grade team? Boy, could he hit! I'll never forget the crack of the bat as it connected with the ball every time. But now, the only sports he can play are in his head. When Hank listens to games on the radio, he forgets he can't move his legs and pretends he's his old self again. That's just it, though, it's all pretend.

Mom wants me to spend more time with my friends, but I know how much Hank looks forward to my visits. I feel so guilty if I don't come by. When I go to the movies with my friends, I feel like I shouldn't enjoy myself. After all, what fun does Hank have in that iron prison? I tell myself I go to the movies to see the newsreels, to write articles for the school paper. It's like I can't allow myself to just enjoy the movie. Not when Hank's been through so much. I know I'm protective of Hank, but golly, he can't even breathe on his own. Sometimes I hate all this. I wish things were back the way they were—before Hank got sick.

Your friend,

Catherine

Pearl Harbor, Hawaii

November 13, 1940

Dear Catherine,

I can't wait until you get here! I told Mother and Dad right away. Gordo's announced to one and all that his best friend, Hank, is coming. Hank's such a good sport to put up with this hero worship.

I can walk to the tennis courts right next to the hospital. I've been playing almost every day, but I miss my favorite doubles partner. Hurry up and get here! I need your help to discourage all these grown-ups who think I'm going to grow up to be just like Mother.

You know the drill the first weeks at a new base. Lots of official visits, shaking hands, and being polite. Last week, when the officers and their wives visited us, I must have heard ten times, "What a lovely girl. Is she going to train to be a nurse?"

I cringed as I heard Mother's stock answer, "Our Meredith could do worse than join us in the medical field or in the Navy."

I faked smiles and shook hands with beautiful officers' wives and pretended to listen. I did okay until this one woman, Mrs. Eagleton. She kept pestering me about my nursing plans and asked thousands of questions. She insisted I come to her house Tuesday night to roll bandages for the war effort in England. Her daughter, Gwendolyn, who's my age, will be there. Mother answered for me and said I'd come. I hate it when she does that.

No, I don't want to be a nurse. And I don't want to be in the Navy. Unless, of course, they'll let me be a pilot. But no women can do that now. And roll bandages? That's just more of the same nursing junk Mother wants me to learn.

Come Tuesday, Mother dropped me off at Mrs. Eagleton's home with strips of cotton cloth and her best surgical scissors. Mrs. Eagleton introduced me to everyone as "the daughter of Captain

William J. Lyons, that new surgeon at the hospital, and the lovely Navy nurse, Marilyn Lyons." The women all ooohed and aahhhed. Here it comes, I thought.

"Meredith's going to study to be a nurse too." Inwardly I groaned, but I replied, "Nice to meet you," and took a seat at the dining room table at the farthest end from Mrs. Eagleton, next to the only other girl my age. I plopped my basket of cloth strips on the table.

"I wanted to be a nurse too," Mrs. Eagleton's daughter, Gwendolyn, said. "One day I volunteered at the hospital, but the smells just didn't agree with me."

"It's not for everyone," I replied. Gwendolyn's beautiful. She has long curly red hair and a few perfect freckles across her perfect nose. I stared at her sitting there in her freshly ironed dress. She looked every bit an officer's daughter. Not at all like me. Give me a ponytail and a tennis outfit any day. As Gwendolyn rolled her bandages, I stared at her long slender fingers and painted nails. I curled my fingers to hide the two broken nails from my tennis game.

Mrs. Eagleton jingled a small handbell she kept by her place. An Asian woman, head down, handed fruit punch drinks to everyone. She backed out of the room with her empty tray still held high and gave little nods as she disappeared into the kitchen. Mrs. Eagleton asked, "Has your mother found a maid yet, Meredith? She simply cannot make it here without good help. Not with two children and her duties, you know."

I didn't know. We'd gotten along fine so far, it seemed to me.

"The Jap girls are the best. Why, I've never had a bit of trouble with mine. I check my jewelry after every time she's here. So far, she hasn't taken a thing." Can you believe that pompous old bat said that? Then she said, "I'll get your mother a reference right away. You can't be too careful these days — with the war coming and all."

"Why, I've never had a bit of trouble with mine." So are they some kind of possession? I think not. They're people! They've got names! "You can't be too careful these days." Yeah, like right now. I think I need to be careful who I associate with. Geez, Louise, these people are opinionated! I sure hope Mother doesn't get a maid. If she does, she'd better not call her "her girl."

Gwendolyn made the night bearable and filled me in on the dances, the boys, and the teachers at Roosevelt High. I started school there the next day. Her boyfriend is a football star. Figures. At the end of the evening, I had stacks of rolled bandages and was exhausted from being nice to Mrs. Eagleton. You'll have to thank me later for going through all this first! Hurry and get here. I need someone normal to talk to.

Your friend,

Merrie

Adventures in Jamestown
Softcover • ISBN 9780310713920

Londoner Abigail Matthews, a daring adventurer, moves to Jamestown
and then Henricus, Virginia, where she comes to know Pocahontas, who
was captured by the settlers. Her best friend Elizabeth Walton, still in
England, encourages Abigail to see past her hurt and anger to befriend
this most unlikely of companions. Excellent for educators and homeschool use.

Secrets of Civil War Spies

Softcover • ISBN 9780310713906

As the United States is torn apart in the early days of the Civil War,
two girls risk everything for what they believe to preserve the Union.
Emma, a Yankee, finds creative ways to keep her identity secret, while
her southern friend Mollie must decide if she, too, will spy on the
Confederacy. Excellent for educators and homeschool use.

Available now at your local bookstore!

Attack at Pearl Harbor
Softcover • ISBN 9780310713890

Determined to learn to fly, Meredith experiences consequences that
will unwittingly provide her just what she needs when the Japanese
bomb Pearl Harbor in 1941, and her best friend's determination to
report on unfolding events puts her family right in the center of the
story. Excellent for educators and homeschool use.

Available now at your local bookstore!

We want to hear from you. Please send your comments about this book to us in care of zreview@zondervan.com. Thank you.